Sunset
By Belinda Topan

ISBN: 978-0-9943500-3-9

Any references to historical events, real people, or real places are used fictitiously. Names, characters, and locations are products of the author's imagination. Information cited is used to explain the story and the purpose of particular events to help the reader understand.

Front cover image by Belinda Topan
Book design by Belinda Topan

Artwork Created by Puppypaww

Twitter: https://twitter.com/puppypaww
Website: https://puppypaww.carrd.co/

Proof Reading and Editing was done by Sundus
Fivver Username: Sundus_writings

Ebook publishing with Amazon
First printing edition 2021.
www.belindatopan.com.au

Thank you

First off I just want to say thank you, dear reader, for purchasing a copy of this book.

I also wish to extend my thanks to the online readers who have been here since the first page of living with vampires and have continued reading my other works. I also wish to thank Sundus Writings for editing my Novel and Puppypaww for drawing my characters.

I hope you enjoy the story before you and have a chance to look at my other stories.

Happy reading!

Glossary

BCE – Before Common era (Scientific term for BC)
CE – Common Era (Scientific term for AD)

(Ludus latrunculorum , 2006) – Ludus latrunculorum, latrunculi, or simply latrones ("the game of brigands",

from *latrunculus*, diminutive of *latro*, mercenary or highwayman) was a two-player strategy board game played throughout the Roman Empire. It is said to resemble chess or draughts, but is generally accepted to be a game of military tactics. Because of the scarcity of sources, reconstruction of the game's rules and basic structure is difficult, and therefore there are multiple interpretations of the available evidence.

Bibliography

Ludus latrunculorum . (2006, November 18). Retrieved from Wikipedia the free encyclopedia: https://en.wikipedia.org/wiki/Ludus_latrunculorum

6 BCE (Before Common Era)

"I see it!" the old warlock declares, flaying his arms up in the air. The hot cauldrons of fire burst, shooting up a river of flames. The emperor stands still as his people quickly back away in fear.

He draws a shaky breath. Stiffly watching the dark magic the warlock has used.

Blood only pools from the altar. The smell of burning flesh clutches to the thick smoky air, making it impossible to breathe.

The few lives of his people will be worth the sacrifice.

"What do you see?" the emperor asks. Proud to keep his voice steady in front of a power-hungry warlock.

"The gods have given me a vision. A vision of a boy!" the warlock swiftly turns to the emperor. The servants and guards back away. Small gasps and shrills are heard amongst the temple. "Yes, a boy. Born in the second Sanguine." The warlock announces. Carefully stepping down the altar, trying not to slip over the blood.

"Did you get a name?" the emperor asks drearily. Getting tired of the warlocks performance. As a child, he has put up with old coots nonsense, and for years he has tolerated him for his dramatics. The emperor has only kept him at his royal court because he is the only one to use Decay magic.

"No – no – no," he mutters to himself, turning away from the emperor. Tapping his chin and shaking his head uncontrollably, he mutters to himself like a lunatic. "But Wait!" he jumps back, causing a fright for everyone within the room. "I do have a plan."

The emperor sighs in relief. Finally, getting results.

"But you will not like it."

The emperor frowns. Taking a deep breath, he stares into the delusional warlock's eyes. His eyes are turning a milky white.
"What is it?"

****

It was an early morning for Alexandros. Never have the chance to get a decent amount of sleep or rest. It is the same tedious routine, having to force himself out of bed, stumble across the empty space of his home, to the spare room, and soothe the trembling young child inside.

He always did want a son or daughter. He didn't really care what gender they were, he just wanted a family, but of course, he never had this in mind.

It is to be expected. Alexandros thought to himself.

Quietly sitting on the edge of the bed, Alexandros wraps the small boy into a hug. The child was trembling, tears streaking down his face and wetting his night tunic.

It needed to be washed anyway. Alexandros thought, watching the boys snot wipe into the cream-coloured fabric.

"Another nightmare?" Alexandros asks the boy. The brown-haired child nodded, sniffling.

"They killed me," he whispers. "I could feel their spears piercing into me as I begged to be let go," he trembles, salty tears begin to leak from his eyes once more.

Alexandros said nothing but held the boy closer, humming a tune, his love used to sing to him during their long journeys.

He felt sorry for the boy, having to lose so much in such a short time. Now to be troubled in his sleep, the gods are ruthless. The boy has dreamt of how he died in so many different ways. He is waking up every night, screaming, begging for it all to go away.

Alexandros asks himself if he has done the right thing. Saving this boy from the same fate as all those children had faced.

Death. It's everywhere. The streets run with blood, the air is filled with the scream of desperate mothers trying to protect their children. And I, in the midst of it all, can only save one boy.

He was running in the forest outside the city. He was lucky to escape the city walls, even more, lucky to run into Alexandros.

This madness came in the early hours of the morning, two months ago. Awoken by the terrors within the night, the smell of burning flesh. Alexandros thought the worse when he jumped out of his bed, hoisting his sword from the floor and run towards the city. He expected vampires or witches to be causing mayhem. His heart only sunk when he laid eyes on the poor boy on the dirt ground, bleeding from his knees and the royal guards charging for the boy.

No one was expecting the onslaught of the royal guard that night. They all fought back but miserably failed and only watch in horror as their sons were killed. Daughters were spared, older brothers lived, so did the babies.

Boys born in a specific year were slaughtered. Alexandros was filled with rage as he hears the orders given out to the guards. They did not enjoy nor agree, but it had to be done.

Alexandros marched to the royal grounds, the boy clinging on to his robes for dear life. Not once did he let go, fearing that he would be put up for the slaughter once he did.

Alexandros could not save all the boys in Rome, it was too late for him to take any action, but it would be this boy if he could save one life tonight.

The emperor is a reasonable man. He would not have caused such an order without reason. Even if there was a valid reason, this was not the right way to go.

Fury bubbled beneath the surface as he marched up the stone steps, the guards trailing close behind. Nothing would stop Alexandros from getting to the emperor and throwing the first punch upon his old friend. The guards around him went ballistic as he did, but of course, the man he called friend only sighed and getting back from the ground.

Alexandros sighs at the memory. He remembers such sadness in his friend's eyes. The emperor knew what he had ordered is wrong, he knew the devastation it had brought upon his people, but it was the only solution he and the deranged wizard had.

The boy would cling to him closer as the wizard lays his milky white eyes upon the boy, screaming incoherent mumblings of a mad man and pointing at the small child with his long spindly fingernails.

"It's you. You will be a devastation to us all! He will kill us. He is the bringer of death! Kill him! Kill him before he grows up!"

Alexandros had to be there for a few minutes before shutting the old man up with his fist.

"I'm asking as a friend," Alexandros's eyes stay upon the wizard, clutching his injured jaw. Waiting for another excuse to punch the old man for suggesting such a heinous act. "Let me look after the boy, and if this deranged old fool is correct, I will put an end to him myself."

Alexandros regrets those words now, but he knew it was the only way to save the boy, a false promise to the emperor, but they do not know that.

The boy was fearful of him, conflicted with the man who saved him but promised to kill him later. The boy only wonders if he should run away at this point.

Alexandros cursed his name and begged the gods for forgiveness. He does not wish harm, nor did he want to destroy this boy's trust. But what choice did he have?

The boy's parents are gone, trying to save him during the slaughter, and word of his older brother getting adopted by a wealthy family since they have only daughters. The boy would have died that night if Alexandros had not stepped in.

Alexandros looks to the window and watches the sun slowly rise over the horizon. Birds begin to sing. Once covered in darkness, the light shines over the land to give a brilliant colour of green and the sky a beautiful orange. This is the other reason why Alexandros doesn't mind getting up so early.

The boy shifts and stirs before opening his hazel eyes.

"Good morning, Alexandros," he whispers.

"Good morning Syrus."

Silent

Syrus is a quiet boy, too quiet. Quiet as a mouse, in Alexandros's opinion. He has, on many occasions, unintentionally scare Alexandros. Alexandros believes he is alone and only turns around and is faced with a hazel-eyed boy staring at him.

He has learned to grow weary of Syrus's sudden appearances, but there are times he is caught off guard.

Syrus would only speak when spoken to. He watches Alexandros with great curiosity as he grows the crops they eat, watch him train, and listen to every word the man has to say. Alexandros would speak of his adventures, how to grow plants during the seasons, and take your opponent down without seriously harming them. All are useful – well, the stories not so much, but everything else is a lesson for Syrus to learn.

Syrus finds Alexandros to be an interesting man. He is not like the rest of the people in the city of Rome. Taking note, Alexandros lives on the outskirts of the city, building his home with his own two hands, alongside his lover.

Syrus has also questioned whether Alexandros is closely related to a boar. Considering the thick black hairs covering his skin, all over his broad chest, arms, legs, thick black curly hair on top of his head, and thick bushy eyebrows. Syrus is thankful it's not on his back. He has enough nightmares to deal with.

Overall, Syrus is thankful for Alexandros's intervention. He would not be here, watching the older man grow their food.

"Syrus, fetch me some water from the well, will you?" Alexandros asks.

Without a word, Syrus nods his head and walks to the makeshift well Alexandros has built. Syrus helps where he can. Whether it be fetching water or trying to till the soil, he wants to help. It's the least he can do.

Syrus runs over to the makeshift well, grasping the wooden handle and tieing the rope around before throwing it into the well. Syrus hears the bucket fall with a loud clang before crashing into the depths. It didn't sound like crashing into the water but more like the wood smashing into the ground to Syrus. Syrus begins pulling on the wire rope. The bucket is lighter than he anticipated.

The wooden handle comes into view, but nothing is left of the wooden buckets he threw a few seconds ago. It swings in the air, laughing at Syrus. He will have to be the bearer of bad news to Alexandros.

Slowly he makes his way back to the house. Alexandros is tilling away and planting the seeds.

Swallowing the non-existent spit, Syrus timidly shuffles towards Alexandros, and nervously playing with his fingers and staring down at his dirtied feet.

"Where's the water boy?" Alexandros asks Syrus, tiredly leaning against the hoe. Syrus scarcely looks into his eyes. His lips waver as he opens his mouth.

"There's no water. The bucket broke when it went into the well," Syrus finally replies but flinches away and closes his eyes. Waiting for Alexandros to explode at the boy.

Alexandros had never shown any aggression before. He couldn't exactly understand where this fear had initially come from. He wants Syrus to trust him, to believe he would bring no harm to the boy, but that will only take time.

Sighing tiredly, Alexandros straightens up and walks to the house. Syrus stays frozen in place as he watches the older male come back with two large wooden buckets.

"Looks like we need to head into the city, where the fountain is," Alexandros passes Syrus a bucket and carries the other. Without another word, Syrus silently follows the older male into the city.

Syrus clutches the bucket closer to his chest. Memories of the past flash before him. He can still hear the screams of the city, his mother begging the guards to let him go, his father dying before him, and his brother cursing his name as he is dragged away from the corpses of their parents as they lay dead in the street.

The boy takes a shaky breath, focusing on the smell of animal manure and dry dirt mixed around in the humid air. His body shakes as they continue on their onset path for water. The streets become busier, people from all over to sell their goods, animals caged or tied to a post, children running rampant on the streets. Syrus felt more unease as they step deeper into the city. He can hear the cries of mothers screaming for their children, demanding they get inside, ignoring the child's protest.

Syrus can feel it, their wary eyes, their silent whispers, the noise dulls as the people watch both Alexandros and Syrus make their way through. He can only beg it is for Alexandros and not the boy who survived the massacre, but life is not kind.

"How dare you," both Syrus and Alexandros stop in their tracks as a woman comes marching from her home. Her face reddening as she comes closer, her eyes welling up. "How dare you bring this thing here!" she screams at Alexandros but points to Syrus. Syrus freezes in place, his eyes pop from his head as he looks at the woman's finger. "I lost my son because of him!"

Fury begins to bubble within Alexandros. The colour red only begins to blur his vision.

"He had nothing to do with this. If you want someone to blame, blame that foolish wizard!" Alexandros screams back.

"He's one of them, he's the predicted monster, all has been lost because you refuse to let him die. My son's life has been sacrificed in vain due to your selfishness."

The crowd becomes riled and agrees with the woman, many yell and scream at them, blaming Alexandros and Syrus.

"I say we kill the boy right now!" one man screams, and they all come to an agreeance.

The same makes a grab for Syrus, but Alexandros was quick and jumped into action. Syrus's feet flew off the ground, his body held firmly by the hairy boar man, and he watches the screaming mob grow smaller and smaller as they make their quick escape.

Syrus knows how pointless it is to follow two people through the city. It is like a maze with so many twists and turns, making it easy for any man and child to hide in its cracks crevices.

Alexandros slumps down on the dusty ground, painting against the wall in the dim alley. Syrus clings on to dear life, shaking in Alexandros's hold, his heart ramming out his chest, his breathing fast-paced and uncontrollable.

Alexandros tried his best to soothe the shaking child, just holding the boy close and letting him cry it all out.

Syrus didn't want to walk back out to the open. He didn't want to face the cruel mob waiting for them both. Yet Alexandros was determined to go out and get water, it shouldn't be this much of a challenge, yet here they are, sitting in the dirt, hiding.

Alexandros would have taken them on if he did not have to worry about the boy.

Heaving a sigh, Alexandros removes the weeping boy from his arms, carefully placing his two bare feet on the ground.

"All right, I will get the water, and you stay here," Syrus nods his head, sniffling as he goes along.

Alexandros leaves Syrus alone in the alley. The boy stays quiet, replaying the moments before over and over in his head. They see him as a monster. They blame him for all the children murdered in cold blood and painted it to be some noble sacrifice if all the children had died. But his life, the only soul to remain, had made it all mute for the people in this city.

He didn't ask for this. He didn't ask for any of it.

"Thought I might find you here," Syrus looks up from the soil and finds himself, face to face with his own flesh and blood.

"Pietro," Syrus croaks, relief filling him as he lays eyes upon his brother, believing he had lost him to the chaos two months ago. Running towards his older brother with arms wide open, ready to embrace his own family once more, but this reunion isn't happy.

Syrus was knocked back by Pietro's fist coming into contact with his cheek. It throbbed from the blow with a painful sting when Syrus went to reach his cheek. He flinches as he made contact.

Syrus leaves his mouth hanging. Words get stuck in his throat as he looks up to his brother. His fists are clenched, eyes burning with deep hatred, jaw tightly clenched.

"It's all your fault," Pietro seethes. "You killed our parents. If it wasn't for you, they'd be still alive!" Pietro screams at him, point the finger right at Syrus.

Syrus opens his mouth, but nothing comes out. He wanted to protest, reason with his brother, explain this wasn't his doing. He didn't ask for any of this to happen.

Pietro stalks closer to the younger boy, ready to lash out at Syrus once again. Even if Syrus attempted to escape, he wouldn't know where Alexandros would be, the guards would have found him, they also kill him on the spot, no one would help Syrus. He would only pray to the gods, begging them to hear his plea and hope Alexandros comes back in time.

"Hey!" the blows from Pietro's fists stop coming. Syrus is left with the dull ache from his body as he tries to shield himself at best.

Syrus blearily watches his older brother run off in the other direction and Alexandros lifting Sryus from the hard ground. Panic fills the older male as he looks upon the beaten boy, thankful it was another child, knowing the wounds would be far greater if it had been from an adult. "Why didn't you call for help?" Alexandros snaps.

"It was too risky," Syrus murmurs in Alexandros's arms. The man is still unsure of what to make from the boy's words. "If I called, I would be dead before you came back. I had to wait for you," Syrus clarifies, and everything fell into place.

It's sad enough Syrus had suffered already, but to know his place in this world and to accept his existence, this boy knew his life will always be in danger from the vengeful citizens of Rome. The boy who should have died, the monster, the reason why they had lost so many lives that night. They curse his existence and will do anything to be rid of him.

Alexandros's heart breaks and curses the gods above. *"Please spare this boy."*

Annabeth

Alexandros no longer took Syrus into the city with him – well, more, Syrus refused to go in and made Alexandros promise never to do that again. He's an intelligent child, too bright for Alexandros's liking. It is only just now that Alexandros has noticed how different Syrus is compared to previous children he has met. Keeping his mouth shut that day when entering the city ins one of them. But there are other moments Alexandros has witnessed. He has watched Syrus assess situations, and problem solve by himself to overcome these situations.

Many older students he had taught over the years were never as bright as Syrus is, even at the age of four. He has watched the boy lure a donkey onto the small field they own with a carrot and use the donkey to till the ground. All but using the rope and the hoe and tying it to the donkey. Impressive none, the less but Alexandros wonders where he got the donkey from.

He's begun teaching the boy to read but didn't expect him to pick up on it so fast. He would often watch Syrus leave the house with a few books, wandering into the small forest close by. He would return later that evening, asking Alexandros what certain words were and what they meant. Syrus became more complex as he came across a book with math equations, another subject the boy has adapted to. Alexandros has always been a big believer in education. He never looks down upon those who wish to seek knowledge.

Syrus, on the other hand, has found it to be a good distraction.

Though he usually wanders away from the house, he finds himself sitting on the front porch in the shade today. Syrus can make the days go quicker when he reads, getting lost in the old history of his city. He yearned to be part of it, to be accepted by the people, but he knows this day would never happen.

With all the books in Alexandros's library, there is one book Syrus's is enraptured by. He doesn't recognize the handwriting. He struggles to read their writing, finding it hard to understand what they write, but one name sticks out. 'Alexandros.' The person mentions him frequently throughout the book, but Syrus is still yet to decipher the rest.

Putting the book down, he closes his eyes, rubbing the temples of his head. It ached and throbbed within his skull. *I think that's enough reading for one day.*

Syrus forces his eye open as he hears the quiet neigh in the wind. Horses are usually close by when the guards are near. It is unusual for them to be here. Alexandros patrols the area and takes his word when it is clear. Plus been known as the demon spawn, everyone tends to stay away.

Six guards surround one man on horseback, all armed to the teeth, swords wielded and ready at a moment's notice. Syrus is quick to jump to his feet. All the guards stare at the young boy, pointing their weapons at the child. He freezes, watching the sharp points of the blades coming closer to him.

"Alexandros!" Syrus's voice quivers while shouting. The older gentleman rushes out the door, hair dishevelled and tunic just barely clinging to his body. Syrus is thankful he achieved to rush out with clothes in such a short amount of time. Alexandros clears his throat and slicks back most of his unruly hair. "General."

The man on horseback nods to the unruly man, nudging the horse's sides and clop closer to the house. Upon closer inspection, the general wears fine Egyptian cotton, golden rings adorn his finger, a broad sword hoisted on his hip, also ready for battle.

"Sir Alexandros," the older man greets. "I'm sorry for intruding, but I am searching for my daughter," the general explains.

Syrus hears rustling in the bushes nearby, his eyes wander over, a dark silhouette comes to light. His eyes pop open, a young girl with long brown wavy hair and olive skin. She puts her finger on her light pink lips. Syrus swallows and looks away from the girl in the shrubbery. Returning his attention back to the grown-ups.

"I haven't seen a young girl. I have been inside all morning. Syrus, have you seen anyone?" all eyes direct to the young boy. He shrinks back to the brick wall and shakes his head. Alexandros sighs but shrugs. "We can offer our assistance to help find your daughter?"

"I would greatly appreciate it, but that thing must stay here." Syrus knows who they mean and bows his head to the ground, staring at his sandals.

Alexandros held back the hurling insults, grinding his teeth and accepts, nothing more than to rid of this man.

The guards and general begin marching forward. Alexandros gives Syrus one last look. "I'll be back soon, ok."

Syrus nods and watches them all leave, wandering deeper into the woods. Syrus looks back to the shrubbery, noticing the young girl is now gone. Syrus sighs to himself and turns back to the pile of books waiting for him – or were waiting for him. Gone, all three, gone. Rustling is heard once more but within the house.

Syrus's heart leapt from his chest. He no longer desired to go inside and escape the heat. He would happily be out in the wild than deal with whatever is inside.

"Hey," a voice from inside whispers. Syrus leaps back from the house, shaking like a leaf in the wind. A head pops up from the window, startling Syrus and falling to the ground landing heavily on his butt. He winces from the pain, rubbing the area he landed on. The same girl from the bushes giggles but is quick to be by Syrus's side.

"Sorry about that," she giggles again, putting her hand out for Syrus.

He stares at the hand, unsure what to do at this point. The thoughts in his head raced through many scenarios, telling him how each one can go wrong. The young girl furrows her brow, her emerald green eyes staring at the boy. She moves her hand closer to him. "I'm not going to hurt you," She insists.

Syrus hesitates, lifting his hand off the ground, slowly inching his own hand to the girls. She patiently waits, like how you would feed a skittish doe bread from your hand, quiet, still, and patient. Syrus grabs the girl's rough hand and is hoisted from the ground. She gives the boy a broad smile, exposing her pearly white teeth. "See, told you."

Syrus gives the girl a weak smile in response, but this wasn't good enough for her. She looks around, making sure it was still the two of them.

"You wanna play a game?" she asks the boy eagerly, but Syrus could not give an answer, for his hand had been captured and is dragged through the forest. To avoid falling on his face, Syrus allowed this to happen – or did he? "I know this really cool place, a great way to play some games, we could play ball there it's so big, and no one can find us, it took me forever to get it perfect," she rambles on, uncaring if Syrus was listening or not.

If anything, he was too enraptured by the warmth of her hand. The golden streaks of her hair glistening in the sun, blending beautifully with her chocolate brown and her dazzling green eyes, brighter than the green fields in the hills. Although she is beautiful to Syrus, it was not the most important thing about their interaction. Her smile, her willingness to help him up and take his hand, she did not shudder at his existence or fear that he may curse her. She saw a friend, another child to play with, and to Syrus that made his heart swell with joy.

She drags the boy to a clearing within, a small ball in the centre, and a poorly drawn circle around it. She giddily pulls Syrus through the low thick shrubbery before letting go of his hand and racing to the ball.

"Do you know how to play?" she asks the boy, but Syrus stays silent. Instead, he stands at the edges of the clearing and shakes his head. She frowns again, walking closer to the boy, ball in hand. "I can teach you. It's easy!" She insists. Syrus stays silent but slowly nods his head. She frowns again. "Can't you talk, or do you not want to talk?" she asks him, coming even closer to the boy. Syrus looks at his feet, not wanting to stare into her eyes any longer. He was starting to feel intimidated by her. The girl huffs and drops the ball down, letting it roll to Syrus's feet. "Well, I guess I know the reason," Syrus snaps his head back up to the girl, her arms crossed together. "I haven't told you my name. I'm a complete stranger. You don't know me. That's why you're afraid to talk to me," she smiles triumphantly. Syrus tried to hold back his giggles. He found this all too amusing at the girl's attempt to open him up. She huffs again and puts her hands on her hips, glaring at the laughing boy. Syrus calms himself and takes a deep breath.

"I'm – Syrus," he croaks.

The girl eases, letting her hands fall off her hips and graces Syrus with a smile before saying one word. "Annabeth."

Vampyr

Since Annabeth met Syrus, she has made it her mission to escape her family home and visit the young boy. Much to Alexandros's displeasure, he has accepted this and is willing to assist the girl if needed. They have made a plan, a time, and the number of hours spent here in their little house. As long as Annabeth doesn't get caught, these meetings can continue. It is odd for a young girl to wander away from their male caretaker, but Alexandros can tell the girl is headstrong, and she will not take no as an answer. Her father would always be searching for her or ensure a tighter leash on the girl. Worse comes to worst, she would be kicked out of the home, shunned by her family. Alexandros would take the girl in if it ever came to that.

During the time spent together, Alexandros realised they both seem to learn from each other, Syrus's love for reading has also captured Annabeths attention, and he spared no time helping her read. Which then proceeded to other topics Syrus had begun to learn. He would teach her with giddy excitement and explain how each equation works or the stars created by our gods. Normally women of Rome are never given this opportunity. Still, to Syrus, he didn't see that he saw a friend, an equal, and to Alexandros, that was more important to him than some taboo rule in society.

Annabeth had also helped the boy come out of his shell. They roughhouse out in the gardens, use the dolls she had brought and use them for war tactics. Syrus would use the books for reference. She would win in most physical activities, swordplay, and wrestling, and Syrus had won in tactics, but Syrus did not care. He just wanted to be around her. He notices the flowers she picks, her favourite books, and her favourite toys she brings to the young boy whenever he is sad. Syrus would take the time to work in the small field and till the flowers she loves, growing and nurturing them for her. Even as the years go by, they became inseparable.

At age ten, Syrus has grown taller and lankier, with some muscle on him from his work in the field. He hadn't stepped foot in the city since the incident. Nor did he desire too, much to Annabeth's frustration. She would ask him why, but he dismisses the question and find something else to talk about. He is afraid to tell her the truth, fearful that she would reject him just like all those who did in the city.

"Syrus!" Annabeth cries in frustration. Her voice is echoing in the empty forest. "Why won't you come with me!" she shakes his shoulders. Syrus lets the young woman shake him as he continues to read messy handwriting from the journal. He is already struggling to understand the writing, but her shaking isn't helping either.

"I told you why I'm reading," he replies softly. Syrus can never truly get angry at Annabeth, no matter how much the young woman pesters him. She has been by his side for the last six years, and Syrus would do anything for her.

"But you're always reading," She whines, slumping against his back. She crosses her arms and huffs. Syrus smiles at her frustration. He always found her temper adorable but terrifying. He has unfortunately witnessed how dangerous her anger can get. Alexandros was at the receiving end of her rage. Syrus is thankful he had never had to endure it.

"We could play a game," She offers. "But add a bet into the mix," Annabeth continues. Syrus could feel her grin. This intrigued Syrus, a game but a bet, he could never turn down a game.

"All right," Syrus speaks up, closing the book. "I'll bite. What's the bet?" he places the book on the ground and swivels around to stare into her emerald eyes.

He could never stop looking at her, her beautiful olive skin, her waved hair. The more he stares, the more his heart beats frantically in his chest. His stomach flutters, and he feels sick as he is with her. Syrus is genuinely smitten.

"If I win, you come into the city with me," she smiles. Syrus heart plummets to his stomach. He vowed to never step foot in there again. He is pretty content to live outside, or better yet, be far away from here as possible. "And if you win, I'll help you try to decipher that book you have been working on," Annabeth offers. Syrus honestly considered accepting. This book has been driving him crazy, and he knows Annabeth is better at reading messy writing than him.

He could easily ask Alexandros, but he believes this might be sensitive to the older man. The book was buried in the very back of the small library, hidden underneath clothes, books, and armour. It is not something he wishes to bring up, not yet.

"I accept your terms," Syrus agrees, dread slowly creeping down his spine.

Annabeth hops off the ground and rushes over to the self-made table made out of a fallen tree. Made specifically to play Latrunculi. Two rows of pebbles, different colours, on either side of the board. The goal of the game is to surround the opponent to win. Syrus is perplexed, a tactic game. He always succeeded in those.

Syrus moved to the old tree. He notices Annabeths fiery passion in her eyes, the confident smirk, head held high. Syrus already knew this was a bad idea.

Pebble by pebble, they both play for over an hour, Syrus has been almost cornered a few times, quickly getting himself out of the sticky situations, but in the end, Annabeth has won for the first time.

Syrus let his mouth fall open, his black pebbles surrounded by her white stones. He couldn't fathom the loss. His strategies were superb. He always knew how to outsmart his opponent by one step ahead. Admittedly Syrus is frustrated. He wanted a rematch.

Swiftly snapping his head from the board, determination flowing through his veins, ready for round two – but he didn't. It all melted away when he saw her smile, her little victory dance, cheering the gods up in the sky. Her happiness was far more important than winning.

The boy smiles to himself, gets up from the ground, and holds his hand out to Annabeth. She stops mid-dance and stares at his hand. She frowns, a little confused. Syrus snorts, at her, understanding she had forgotten the bet.

"A deal's a deal remember," he reminds her, still smiling. Annabeth returns Syrus's smile and takes his hand. Their fingers entwine together. Syrus's cheeks burn, turning a little pink, bringing life to his pale skin.

Annabeth leads Syrus from the forest out onto the dirt road. His heart begins to frantically beat as his eyes land upon the city before him. Memories of that unfortunate night rose within. The screams of terror, the smell of burning flesh, blood painting the streets red, all stained in his mind. Syrus stops at the gates, his body shakes, his breathing becomes laboured, bile from his stomach begins to rise into the throat, threatening to spill out from his mouth.

Annabeth stares at Syrus, bewildered. She could have never anticipated this reaction. Annabeth gently squeezes Syrus's hand, and he looks down. Focusing on their entwined fingers, feeling the warmth radiating at their bounded hands.

"It's ok. We don't have to go any further," Annabeth soothes. He swallows and nods frantically, quickly dragging Annabeth in the other direction, away from the cursed city.

"I was wondering what hole you crawled out from," Syrus froze. Dread creeps up his spine, into his stomach once more. He once believed to be safe, he is now in danger. "Syrus, and here I thought you died in a hole somewhere."

Syrus let's go of Annabeth's hand. Keeping his back to them all. Pretending it's just him and no one else in this serene view, but if he turns around, he must face his fear.

"Don't speak to him like that," Annabeth challenges them, and Syrus's heart leaps from his chest.

"Oh," the voice coos. "You're letting a girl defend you! That's pathetic. What kind of vampyr are you," Syrus snaps his head around, fear enriching his eyes as he stares upon Annabeth. Shaking with fear, waiting for her to realize the truth.

"Pietro," Syrus whispers, pleading him to keep his mouth shut.

"What are you talking about?" Annabeth stands tall in front of Syrus, ready to protect the boy.

Pietro and his lackeys laugh. "Don't you know? This freak is one of them, a murderer. He's the reason why those kids died six years ago."

Syrus knew the people called him a monster, a beast. He never knew the creature they related him to until now. Vampyr is a new concept to the boy, and much to his frustration, he has asked Alexandros numerous times why they hate him. What beast do they call him?

"He's human! How can you blame him for something that he had no part of!" Annabeth defends Syrus, but all the boys laugh.

"Oh, but he is. He's the reason why my parents are dead," Pietro hisses and stalks closer to Annabeth. Syrus quickly grab Annabeth's hand. She snaps her head to him. Confused as to why Syrus would hold her.

"Let's just go." He whimpers. Tears are brimming in his eyes.

"You're not going anywhere vampyr," it was at this moment Annabeth had enough. Ripping her arm from Syrus's grasp and throwing a punch at Pietro.

Everyone became silent. Shock gripped their voices, staring in disbelief that a woman struck a man.

Pietro saw red, holding nothing back, struck back, and Annabeth hit the ground. Blood mixed with saliva pools from Annabeth's mouth. She spits out the blood, running her tongue against her teeth, thankful they are still intact. It was at this moment time had slowed.

Something primal within Syrus snaps, stalking towards the older male, the power coursing through him with each step. He can feel the rage rising within his chest. Syrus did not like to fight, but he knew it was necessary. They hurt Annabeth.

Pietro confidently smiles down at Syrus throwing a punch down at the smaller male. Syrus smirks, quickly side-stepping his punch and grab onto Pietro's arm, pulling him closer for Syrus to strike his face. Syrus can hear the sickening crunch from Pietro's nose. The older boy backs away, holding onto his bleeding face. His eyes fill with fear, watching the young boy slowly walk towards him. Something in him changed, and Pietro can see it. Confidence dripping off him, his eyes old and filled with knowledge as if he has lived through centuries. The young smiles at the older boy that send chills down his spine.

Stalking closer to the group of boys, they scramble amongst themselves, turning tail and flee, leaving Pietro behind. Pietro only stumbles backward, falling onto his butt.

"Syrus." Annabeth's voice rings in his head. The boy stopped in his tracks. Becoming aware of his surroundings once more.

Pietro took this opportunity to run away from the two, holding his bloodied nose. Syrus watches his older brother, running away, with his tail between his legs.

***

Annabeth and Syrus return to his house, sitting Annabeth on a stool outside. Syrus retrieves a washcloth from the house ad dipping it into the bucket full of water.

"Are you ok?" Syrus asks Annabeth, wiping the blood away from her face. She nods in reply, moving her lips. They are swollen. Annabeth stops Syrus's hands and grabs the washcloth out of his hand.

"Syrus," Annabeth whispers. "You need to tell me the truth."

King

Alexandros glanced upon the two youths, concerned to find blood on the young girl's face, and Syrus delicately wiped the blood away from her lip. Questions begin to pop up in Alexandros's head. Did they roughhouse too much, did they get into a fight, are they no longer friends?

"Syrus," Annabeth finally speaks up. "You need to tell me the truth."

Ah. Alexandros's heart plummeted. Something must have happened to incur such a question. Alexandros steps into the clearing, both children startle as Alexandros makes his presence known. Syrus quickly steps away from Annabeth, bowing his head to the ground. Alexandros knows this stance. Syrus curls up inside himself, believing he is to blame for the situation and bring grief upon his loved ones. He did this a lot when he was younger. It's to make him look small and weak, not wanting to cause further trouble.

"All right, what happened?" Alexandros asks them both.

***

All three are inside the tiny home, the silence leaves anticipation between the elder and the two children, waiting for Alexandros to begin his story. Alexandros heaves a sigh, getting up from his chair and grabs the journal Syrus has tried to read over the years. His fingers slowly trace over the cover of the book, his eyes sadly reminiscent.

"This book is a journal. It once belonged to my husband," Alexandros gives a sad smile and opens to the middle of the page. "Terrible writer, no matter how well I taught him to write. But he recorded all of our journeys within this journal," he explains sadly. With another deep breath, Alexandros looks to Syrus. "We both hunted vampyrs, and through the empire, our efforts have not gone unnoticed," Alexandros clears his throat. "Vampyrs are creatures with a human face, they feast on the blood of the living, and they can't be killed through usual methods. They don't age, and mortal wounds cannot harm them. I won't explain what we went through. I'll let you figure the journal out, but when I lost my love, I returned to this city six years ago," Syrus felt a chill go down his spine. He knows where this is going. He looks over to Annabeth, who is intently listening to Alexandros. "There's this mad warlock who is in the emperor's court, using Decay magic and slaughtering people to gain dark knowledge of the universe. He is given a number and a year, nothing more, and yet, somehow they took his words like gospel, and the emperor agrees to the heinous act," Alexandros clears his throat, trying to find the right words. "It was only a hundred years ago the previous king died. In these last hundred, we have been trying to wipe out the vampire species. Out of fear and desperation, many were seeking a solution to predict the next heir, as they fear if he rises, vampires have a fighting chance," Alexandros solemnly explains.

"Is that why the massacre happened so many years ago," Annabeth butts in, the dots finally clicking into place. Alexandros nods his head, grimacing at the memory.

"Syrus is the only child to survive from the predicted year, and since he is the lone survivor, they blame him, curse his name to the gods for he is the supposed king. The fools, if anyone is to blame, it's that crazy warlock," Alexandros growls.

Syrus stares at his hands, currently holding tight onto his tunic, his knuckles turn white, heart pounding from his chest, fear rolling off in waves, he couldn't stop shaking. Memories of the night flash before his mind. His parents lay dead, blood pooling from their bodies, his brother taken away from the guards, and Syrus running, hiding, leaving the city, been chased.

"That's ridiculous," Annabeth hisses, snapping Syrus from his disturbing thoughts. His mouth is left open as he stares at his friend. The fierce determination and frustration mixing together in her eyes. "They have no right to treat him this way. He did nothing wrong," Syrus's chest feels tight. His own heart felt like it was breaking. No one other than Alexandros has vouched for him and heard her speak, as he is a person. Syrus's admiration for the girl continues to grow.

"I hear you, and calling him a vampyr isn't helping either. They truly believe his survival has only happened because he is to be the next king. Not like I had anything to with it," Alexandros adds bitterly, crossing his arms.

Syrus shakes, rage finally bubbling to the surface, the truth coming to light, the reason why they hate him so much.

"I'm not like them," both eyes direct to the young boy, tears leaking from his eyes streaking down his face. "I'm not a vampyr, and I'm not this king the claim me to be," Syrus bites out, clenching his jaw tightly as possible, trying to gain control of his emotions. "I'm human, nothing else." He shouts and storms into his room, taking the journal with him. he shuts the door, and the wind blows a few candles out and echoes through the house.

Alexandros sadly looks to Annabeth. She sits there stunned, not sure what to make of this outburst. Never has she seen Syrus act like this before. Alexandros can only heave a sigh and take Annabeth back home into the city, leaving the boy in the house alone.

Syrus needed to process the information he is given, strained by bitter thoughts of those who are cruel to him. Wiping the tears away from his eyes, sniffling his nose and wiping away the dribble leaking from his nostrils. His chest aches where his heart lays. It softly hurts the boy feeling it beat with each breath he takes. With utter desperation, Syrus snaps open the book, his eyes blurry from the tears. He wipes them away again, trying to read the passages.

It was only after a few minutes more and wiping away tears that Syrus understood something.

'We come across many vampyrs in our journeys, out all the vampyrs we have slain, they are feral with not a single intelligent thought. Eyes brightly red, clawed like hands, mouths always coated with dried blood. I was lead to believe that due to the king's absence, they have returned to a primitive form, but today, something interesting happened. In our hunt, we came across two vampyrs, hunting together, targeting a lone traveller on the roads. These killings are similar to ones we have encountered previously but have never been able to catch them until now. They follow the roads and kill sparingly. Vampyrs are known to feed daily, or they starve otherwise.

Their eyes were nearly white when we encountered them, apparent signs of hunger as they struggle to retract their fangs. Even as we fought, they did their best to protect one another, which is odd, as they always abandon the other just for survival, but they held on till the very end. Even as we successfully killed one, the other stopped. I have never seen such sorrow from these creatures, agony other than hunger. Tears were also spilled. The beast only gave a hysterical laugh and fall to his knees. He doubles overs over grieving for his other half. This was the first time I have ever hesitated to kill a vampyr. I wanted to ask questions, understand what was happening. It even begged to die as life to him wasn't worth living anymore. Alexandros had to commit the finishing blow.

It shook me to the core that night. I have never seen these creatures grieve or spare an emotion to their own kind before. Maybe I am looking at them in the wrong way. They may not just be mindless beasts after all.'

Syrus's chest tightens. The lump in his throat only grew out of proportion. His breathing becomes shaky, nose and eyes uncontrollably leak from his face. He does everything in his power to not let the looming sadness overcome him, but the passage from the journal overwhelms him, gripping his throat, suffocating him. Sobs wracked through his body, and Syrus throws the journal across his room. The book landed on the ground with a heavy thud. Syrus could no longer contain himself. His body shakes as he violently cries. His stomach flips and tightens, making him physically sick. He could no longer hold himself, only to be lost within his emotions.

It has to rain first before you grow

Alexandros has grown increasingly worried about Syrus in the coming days. Since discussing the events in Syrus's past and why they claim a bounty on the boys head, he has refused to leave his room. He barely eats. He lust lies in his bed and ignores the outside world. Alexandros has tried everything in his power to help the boy, but yet he feels helpless as he looks down at the small child, curled up in his sheets. Alexandros wonders if he is too soft and should give Syrus a dose of tough love, but then Alexandros also fears the possibility of resentment from Syrus. It's a predicament that Alexandros feels like he isn't going to win. All he can do is trust his best judgment and hope Syrus can pull himself out of this dark spiel he has dug himself in.

Heaving a sigh, Alexandros leaves the house, closing the door behind him, and wanders into the city alone. With a mission in mind, he wastes no time walking halfway through the city, ignoring everyone's hateful scowls. Syrus is not the only one to cop abuse from the people, but he would have received far worse than Alexandros. Everyone knows not to mess with an experienced vampire hunter.

With deep regret filling his gut and his heart pounding out of his chest, Alexandros never felt this scared in a long time. He shakily knocks on the wooden door three times before it opened. A slave cowers behind the wood. He is clean and well-groomed.

"Is your master in?" Alexandros asks the man. Without a word, he nods and opens the door to let ex hunter in. The slave closes the door and disappears into the depths of the house to retrieve his master.

"Alexandros?" the older man's head snapped towards the familiar high pitched voice. He smiles at

Annabeth, his chest filling with relief. "What are you doing here?" She asks him. Alexandros looks over his shoulder, thankful her father is not here yet.

"I was wondering if you could come with me this afternoon?" Alexandros asks her. Annabeth's eyes widen. Alexandros could literally see the questions popping into her head.

"Is Syrus ok? Is he hurt?" she begins the first two crucial questions as her own heart starts to race.

"He's –," *Fine?* Alexandros cuts himself off, unsure himself. Syrus is ok but not at the same time. There are no physical injuries. "Syrus is . . . Alive," Alexandros puts it lamely. Annabeth noticeably relaxes, releasing the breath she was holding.

"Then what is the matter with him?" she asks, her brow furrowing.

"He hasn't exactly come out of his room," Alexandros weakly explains. Annabeth nods to his words, understanding why the boy has holed himself in there.

"I've been busy with studies, and returning home injured has brought up many questions, but I can sneak out later. Just give me time," Annabeth explains. Alexandros gives the nod to their silent agreement. "Good, I'll see you later," Annabeth quickly rushes away, but before leaving, she provides the slave with a thumbs up. Alexandros looks over his shoulder and sees them nod and smile at the girl. *Smart child.*

***

Syrus knew he was alone in the house once more. It had been days since he last read from the journal, and he had been brave enough to get up from the floor and opening the book once again. Syrus has only come to loathe the people and their hatred in the remaining days, angry at the man who has caused him so much pain, but what can he do? He is but a weak and scared little boy who loves to hide in a book and learn about the outside world. Should he even stay angry? Should he just move on? How can he? So many want him dead.

Syrus's head snaps up as he hears knocking on his door. He takes a shaky breath, his heart sinking a little more. It's probably Alexandros trying to make him feel better again. Syrus didn't want Alexandros. As much as he appreciates it, it's not the person he wants to see. He wants to see her, Annabeth, but Syrus feared she had grown to hate him like the others as the days went by.

"Syrus, it's Annabeth," Syrus's heart leapt from his chest, stumbling to get on his feet and falling onto the floor again and then getting back up to his feet. Syrus stumbles onto the door. His clammy hands grasp the doorknob and open it. There she was, still the same as he last saw her, even the same friendly and beautiful smile. Syrus's mouth became dry as he stares at the girl, taking in all her beauty and the bruise on her lip, giving by Pietro. Rage begins to bubble underneath. She looks away from his gaze and chuckles a little. "Alexandros told me what's been going on," *Of course he has.* "I'm worried about you, Syrus."

Syrus swallows the non-existent spit, his mouth falls open a little as his mind starts to process her words.

"Y-you a-are?" Syrus stutters over his words but managed to get them out. Annabeth looks back to Syrus and smiles once more.

"Of course," Syrus lets go of the breath he was holding and takes another shaky inhale. He moves out of the way and allows Annabeth into his room. She walks in and takes note of the mess, bowls filled with dirty spoons and rotting food, bed sheets strewn across the floor, and cups filled with water.

Syrus also notices this, feels his cheeks burn bright red, and looks away from Annabeth's gaze. She wasn't surprised, considering he has been in here for so long. "I wasn't -," Syrus cut himself off. Right now, his words are not well equipped for this situation.

"It's all right. I'm more worried about you, though. It hurts to know you have disconnected yourself from the world," Annabeth murmurs, walking over to Syrus's bed and sitting herself down. "It must be painful. I'm sorry you have to go through this," Syrus stays silent, already deep in thought. "Just remember, Alexandros and I are always here for you. What happened back then wasn't your fault." Syrus could feel the tears well up in his eyes. As much as he heard this from Alexandros time and time again, the only person he ever wanted to hear it from is her.

It was at this moment, Syrus knew he could never let any harm come towards her again. Even if it were his dying breath, he would keep her safe, no matter the cost. She has given him so much, and she had done little in doing so. To be there, be on his side, believing he is no beast. Syrus swore to himself from this day forward, he will get stronger for her.

"Thank you," Syrus sniffles wiping his nose, and Annabeth gives him a sweet smile.

A solemn oath

In the events leading up to this moment, Syrus is unsure how this would play out. He woke up with a mission, jumping out of bed, marching through the house, outside to find his guardian, and ask – no – demand to learn self-defence.

Alexandros is caught off guard, the hoe slipping out of his hands, the sweat dripping off his forehead, and his mouth going slack.

"You," Alexandros starts, gripping the hoe again. "Want me," he lifts it up in the air, "To teach you," slinging it down to the ground, with such force, the blunt metal digs into the dirt. "How to fight," he pulls back and tills the soil. He heaves out deep breaths and wipes his brow. "You don't like fighting. You back down from violence," Alexandros lifts the hoe again and tills into the soil. "What changed?"

"Annabeth" is Syrus's reply. Alexandros let the hoe slip from his hands again. He stares at the boy dumbfounded, his mouth falls open once more, speechless at the young man. "She was injured because of me. I want to be the one to protect her," Syrus elaborates. Alexandros can see the fire in the boy's eyes, the spark that never existed. Its burns brightly within the boy, a fierce determination to protect the very person he cares for, a fire that Alexandros knows all too well. It is a dangerous flame. As quickly it can spark, it can also go out just as quick.

Alexandros ponders, questioning if he should help feed this fire or let it simmer for a few years, should he doom this poor boy's fate, influencing him to be strong like the warriors in the colosseum, or should he let the boy learn how to fight his battles differently. Any sign of strength and the people of Rome would revolt. Alexandros sighs to himself.

"Is it just for her? Do you have any other reason why you want to learn?" Alexandros asks and watches the boys face conflict, his brow furrow and lips purse together.

"I don't understand," Syrus replies. Hurt mixing with the confident flames within his eyes, they flicker, dulling before reigniting brighter. Alexandros can genuinely see the boy's intentions and understands they are not with malice. Alexandros smirks and affectionately ruffles Syrus's hair.

"You're really doing this all for her, huh?" Alexandros teases, and Syrus slaps his hand away from his hair and huffs. His cheeks begin to burn a bright pink.

"Y-yeah, so?" Syrus spits out, his voice wavering, trying to stay calm, but the boy's heartbeat picks up."I-I just want to ... to ... protect her," Syrus's voice lulls to a whisper. Alexandros understood where the boy is coming from. Syrus is an intelligent young man but is oblivious to the sensation in his chest, how tight and heavy this feeling is, the hot burn within his cheeks. He couldn't understand why his body is reacting the way it is.

"All right, but we have a lot of catching up to do," Alexandros stretches his back and arms. "Boys learn to fight at a younger age, preferably when they start school," Alexandros explains.

"I'm willing to learn," Syrus replies eagerly.

"Oh, I know," Alexandros laughs and ruffles Syrus's hair once more, much to the boys disliking.

***

Syrus has been training vigorously for weeks, Alexandros has not let up on the boy, early morning starts and late finishes in the dark of night, and much to Syrus's disliking, he has had little time to spend with Annabeth. While she is there watching the boy fall on his butt with defeat, after defeat. Annabeth, of course, found this amusing but admired Syrus's determination, willing to get back on his feet, asking what he had done wrong to render his defeat against the older male.

Syrus has attempted to speak with Annabeth on numerous occasions, but Alexandros would put a bud on it. Those small intervals where Syrus thinks training is over and tries to spend time with the girl, Alexandros finds something for the boy to do. It would either be meditation or work on his balance while blindfolded. Some would say it is meaningless – Syrus would definitely think so, considering he knows Alexandros's motives to separate them for the time being. Alexandros knows balance and meditation are essential, but he knows that absence makes the heart grow fonder.

Though she is a partial distraction for Syrus's training, she is also his greatest motivation. Alexandros would stop her coming by if Syrus had not improved, but when she is here, he becomes more focused, determined to grow. Syrus is royally pissed at the older man, but it is necessary to separate them for the time being.

"All right, I think that's enough practice," Alexandros calls out to Syrus – who is currently balancing on one foot and blindfolded. Syrus groaned loudly and put his foot down, and takes the blindfold off. Annabeth giggles at Syrus's displeasure but is proud to see the progress he has made so far. "We'll finish up early tonight. Tomorrow we'll be up before the sun rises," Alexandros smiles at the boy's fallen face. "Annabeth, shall I take you home?"

"That won't be necessary," a voice emerges into the clearing, and a figure comes out from the shadows.

"Father," Annabeth whispers. Annabeth's father stands tall before them, his chest puffed out, his tree-trunk arms crossed over his chest.

"So this is where you have been going to all these years?" he glowers. Annabeth stares at her feet in response. "We are going home, and you will not see this thing again."

"He's not a thing!" Annabeth snaps back at him. Syrus could see the burning rage within her father's eyes, watching him stalk closer to his own daughter and raises a hand. Syrus moves his feet and shields Annabeth from her father's fury.

"Move," the father says with malice.

"I won't let you hurt her," Syrus stands against the firey general. Alexandros is proud but fearful for the boy, ready to step at a moment's notice.

"I am her father, I tell her what to do, and she does it. She needs to know her place in this world," he snarls. Syrus could feel his own anger bubble beneath him, the dangerous rage he had once let out. *Annabeth's place is beside mine.*

"How about we make a deal?" Syrus proposes, and silence befalls all of them. Annabeth's father snaps out of his rage, processing the boy's words, confused about what was just said. "I hear your strategies are legendary. You've won many battles for Rome because of your quick thinking. So how about we make a deal," Alexandros's mouth drops open, Annabeth's breath is caught in her throat, and the general erupts with laughter.

"And what do you propose?" he laughs.

"If I win, Annabeth can see me whenever she pleases, and if I lose, she will never come here again."

"Syrus!" Annabeth snaps, and the father laughs even more laborious.

"All right, I will humour you. You chose the game," The father giggles. Syrus smiles at the older man. He may not be able to take him on one in a fight, but strategy and quick thinking are Syrus's forte.

"A game of Latrunculi," Syrus proposes, and the older man nods his head in agreement.

They stay quiet, playing piece by piece. Both Alexandros and Annabeth watch earnestly, both of them painstakingly quiet as they watch Syrus and the General of the Roman army fight it out in a game of Latrunculi. Alexandros has no doubt of Syrus's intellect, but he worries for the boy, for if he wins, the general may not take his loss lightly, but if Syrus loses, he may never see Annabeth again.

The general's mouth is left open, his eyes widen, and pupils shake as he stares at the board before him. He can't, he couldn't, lose to a mere child, impossible. Could it be the work of some unholy creature, a demon bending this boy will? That must be it. There is no other explanation. The general scrunches his eyes in disbelief until he hears a whisper in the back of his head.

What if he is useful against the enemy? His eyes snap open, looking at the smug child before him. If a child could beat him, then he would be a great asset to Rome's future. The general eases and smiles at the boy. Syrus took this as a threat, his own smile disappearing, ready to fight back.

"Well done," the general puts his hand out. Syrus stares at the general's hand before reluctantly taking it into his own "You're well versed in the game of strategy," he praises Syrus, and they let go of each other's hand. The boy stays silent, glaring at the older man. "Having someone like you would be beneficial for us," The general tsks.

"Yet they all hate me," Syrus glowers.

"That is true, but it's better to have a monster on our side than the enemies. Especially with your mind, we would win every battle. What say, you boy? You won't even have to be on the battlefield and spend time with my daughter as much as you please," he adds to sweeten the deal. Everything about this man is slimy. Syrus gets what he wants and maybe more if he plays his cards right but to leave the safety of his home. The home he has grown accustomed to in the last six years. Syrus sighs to himself and nods. Does he wish to leave the safety of the forest?

"Before I agree, you teach me your strategies, and I complete my training with Alexandros," Syrus bargains. The man frowns, his nostrils flare, and fists tighten. "What's wrong?" Syrus taunts. "Don't you want the glory? To have every battle in the palm of your hands?" Syrus grins at the man before him. Fear tingles in the back of the Generals spine. "Or do you want to fail and remember you had the opportunity to lead this city into greatness, just letting it slip away because you were too prideful to agree to a little boy's terms?"

The General glowers down at Syrus, but the boy did not flinch. Standing his ground and held eye contact with the older male.

"You have guts, boy," he sneers. "I agree to your terms," murmurs, getting onto his feet. "I expect you at my house tomorrow," he orders, but Syrus only shakes his head.

"I have to train with Alexandros, but once it's over, I will visit," the general growls and storms off.

Annabeth stares at Syrus with her bright green eyes, her chest tightens, and her heart heavy as she watches the boy fight in a battle of wills against her father. Her cheeks burn when Sryus returns his gaze to her and smiles.

"I-I'll see you tomorrow," Annabeth blurts out before running to her father, leaving in the darkness. Alexandros just shakes his head and laughs at the two love birds.

Is this love?

Syrus has been working hard under the General of the Roman army and under Alexandros's strict training regime for many years now. No longer he is the string bean boy he once was. At the prime age of sixteen, Syrus's body has toned out, his muscles to his lanky frame. Under his robe, you would not suspect. Though appearances are deceiving, many younger and older boys have tried and failed to win in any fight against Syrus. No longer afraid of the guards' consequences, as they are under strict command to not harm the boy or get involved with these fights. Annabeth's father believes it is good character building for the boy, but he is most impressed when Syrus puts his mind to work. No matter how big or tall the enemy is, Syrus outthinks them, psychs them out, before cleverly pinning them to the ground. It has become known Syrus hates losing.

Annabeth has grown lovelier over the years. Her brown locks have grown past her shoulders, now, hair loosely plaited, hanging over her shoulder. Her childlike features melted away, her cheekbones are sharper, her lips a little plumper, her bosom is far more noticeable, more than Syrus is willing to admit. Shamefully he does stare from time to time but is quick to look away before Annabeth would notice.

He has asked Alexandros about these urges, and the simple reply is, he is becoming a man. Much to Syrus's confusion, he doesn't understand how this makes him a man. Syrus took this upon himself to research what makes him a man, reading from many scholars. Searching through the libraries in the General's private collection, back to his tiny home, searching through Alexandros's library.

Syrus takes note of the old journal he put away a few years ago. He was too emotionally distraught when he first read the passage within the journal, afraid to pick it up again till now.

'Many months had passed since that night. We fought against those two vampires. I tried to reason with every vampire we encounter now. Much to Alexandros's frustration, I still try to make some contact with them. It couldn't be a one-off.

Alexandros did find it odd, but he didn't wish to seek answers as I do, he believes they are all monsters, and not a single thought of reason goes through their heads.

I sometimes still reflect on that night. I remember the grief so vividly in his eyes, the life draining away as he stares at his love. I could imagine the feeling if I ever lost Alexandros myself. I would lose myself in grief just as the vampire did.

I wonder if that makes them more of a man than a monster? Loving is something we humans understand. We consider it a human emotion, and to see a beast have the same feeling, are they indeed monsters?'

Love? Syrus furrows his brow. He has heard of love many times in his life and wonders what it exactly means. He understands it is a different feeling for everyone, but what is love? Is it when he stares at Annabeth's bosom, no? That can't be it, her beautiful features, her eyes? *She has gorgeous eyes.* Syrus smiles at that thought. He could drown in the beautiful sea of emeralds. He does love looking into them when he has a chance. Something in Syrus's chest flutters, this feeling is a regular occurrence much different from the other urge he feels. It's innocent, happy, and it always happens when he thinks of her.

Her smile, laugh, humour, personality, mind, and everything about Annabeth make Syrus's heart soar. *Maybe this is love?* He thinks to himself, with half a smile. Growing up, he feels that life has been a little bit kinder to him, giving him a chance to have some happiness in his life, and Annabeth is definitely the cause of all it. If Syrus hadn't met her, he wouldn't be the man he is today. He wouldn't have given the oath to protect her, to get stronger for her. He would do everything in his power to look after her.

"There you are," Syrus's head snaps up, the melodic voice pulling him from his thoughts. His smile broadens, his heart leaping from his chest. Annabeth is standing over Syrus, her curiousness getting the better of her. She squints at the book's writing but only sighs and sits next to the young man. "In all my years, I still cannot read that messy chicken scratch you call writing," she sighs, her shoulder touching Syrus's as she leans against him.

"I can read it to you," Syrus offers, and a small laugh escapes her lips.

"No, but I have a better idea," Annabeth offers, grasping Syrus's hand and getting up from the ground to pull him up. Syrus's smile grows bigger as she leads him away from the house, where ever Annabeth wanted to go, Syrus will follow. They make their way to the small clearing they used to play at when they were children. Over the years, it has gotten smaller, the bushes and small saplings begin to grow amongst the foliage.

Annabeth finds the old log and the game of latrunculorum still sitting there. The old stones have faded and lost their colour, but still able to see the lines of the patterned board. The wood has twisted and warped a little from harsh elements of the wild. Annabeth let go of his hand and sat on the old log.

"Father told me you have beaten him and every other tactician in a game. I want to see if I can beat you myself," Annabeth smiles, preparing her imaginary army. Syrus sits himself down. Ever since he lost that day against her, he swore not to yield to anyone again. Time went on, and his skills in the game and memory of tactics have improved. But Syrus cannot bring himself to win against her. However, there is one thing Syrus didn't anticipate, how well Annabeth knows him.

Annabeth stares at the old board, her lips pursed, brow furrowing as she stares at Syrus's little stone, surrounded by all her pieces. She should have picked on this sooner, but it was too late when she had finally won the game.

"You lost on purpose," she called Syrus out. Syrus's heart skipped a beat, his cheeks begin to burn up, and he looks away from her accusing gaze.

"I did – not," he weakly responds, but it was a dead giveaway.

"I want a rematch!" Annabeth declares.

"Why? You won?" Syrus argues but knows he will not get his way.

"Because you let me win. I will not leave until you beat me," Annabeth declares and begins assembling the pieces onto the board once more.

"Don't be silly. Take it as a good thing."

Syrus realized he just fucked up. Fury began to bubble over as Annabeth eyes snapped upwards, she could tear him a new one, and he would let her do so. Syrus shut his mouth and let Annabeth draws her face closer to his.

"Never, for a second, let me win, just because you think I am weak. I am not some feeble woman," Annabeth hisses.

"I-I don't," Syrus stammers. Not once did he think that there was something deeper, much deeper, more complicated than to believe she is weak and feeble. She is strong, intelligent, kind, and Syrus loves all those qualities about her. *Love.* Syrus thinks to himself. "I don't see you as weak," Syrus begins. "I never thought you were weak. You're are the bravest person I have ever known. You're brilliant and have a beautiful heart. I would never consider you weak, not for a second."

Annabeth is lost for words at this point. Her fury washes away and felt warm and bubbly on the inside. Her own heart flutters at his words, her cheeks begin to heat up. Not once has anyone said sweet words to her. Many males have tried to woo her, promising her a comfortable life where she can bear children and be looked after. Thankfully her father has never been forced into an arranged marriage and has denied many proposals for her hand. It's as if Annabeth's Father is waiting for something else to occur.

"Well, that's sickening."

Are you a man or a monster?

The sweet moment between Syrus and Annabeth is rudely cut short to a snarky remark.

Pietro stands tall against his brother, his arms crossed, thick like tree branches.

"Why don't you leave that thing and be with a real man Annabeth?" Pietro quips, raising an eyebrow.

"Thank you, but I am not interested," Annabeth hisses. Syrus stands beside Annabeth, ready to step in if things get ugly. She can hold her own in an argument, but in a fight, against someone who has been training all his life, she will not win, and Syrus cannot allow any harm to come to her once again.

Pietro is no fool. Watching the situation unfold, he knows one strike against the fair lady, and he has to answer to Syrus, which is precisely what he wants. He remembers the sting of defeat he experienced so many years ago. Slowly eating away his sanity, as every year passes, Pietro trained to get stronger. Ready to face the thing once more, if it ever dared to shows its true colours. It infuriated Pietro to learn he is in favour of the general of the Roman army. Appalled to hear he, too, has gotten stronger. He wants to tear this whelp apart and claim the girl for his own. Many have tried to win her heart with sweet words. They even try to convince the father to keep her away from the thing, but he relented.

"Now, Annabeth, are you sure?" Pietro coos. "You're standing next to a monster" Pietro voice drips with venom. Syrus steps forward. Annabeth quickly reacted and grabs onto Syrus's arm. He turns his head back to her, eyes pleading with the young man, shaking her head, wishing he would not pursue Pietro. Syrus can understand her worry, but he made a promise. No harm will ever come to her again, even till his last breath.

"I'll give you a chance," Syrus bellows. "Leave," the young man hisses to his so-called older brother. Pietro laughs. It echoes throughout the forest, and the birds flew off scarce.

"Are you challenging me?" Pietro grins, taking a step closer to the two friends. "Cause I still remember the fight we had all those years ago, do you, little brother?" Pietro snarls, taking another step. Syrus remains silent, clenching his jaw tight. He barely remembers that day. Something in him snapped, taking over his entire body and mind. It was Annabeth who brought the boy back to his senses. *I'm not a monster.* "You may have them fooled, but all of Rome still remembers what you are. You're a beast, a monster, a blood-sucking creature!"

Syrus snaps, tackling Pietro to the ground and striking him in the face. The older man just laughs, blood lightly spilling into his mouth, staining his teeth red. Fury pools into Syrus's veins, his vision only trained on the laughing boy. Blinded by anger, Syrus misjudged Pietro's strength and is quickly thrown off. Syrus is now on the ground. Pietro crawls on top of Syrus and begins to throw one punch after another. Syrus desperately tries to throw Pietro off him but is continuously flailed with one blow after another. His face begins to ache and swell all around. Syrus clenches his eyes shut, throwing his arms in the air, and take most of the force. His skin bruises with each fatal blow. Syrus hears Annabeth screaming at Pietro to stop and get off Syrus. Syrus is to blame, giving into Pietro's provocation, so desperate to prove to the world he is no beast. He is still a man, a human, with real feelings.

Pietro grins at the pulverized male, getting off Syrus but kicking his ribs as hard as he can for good measure and spitting on Syrus's arm covered face.

"Not so tough now, are you," Pietro laughs, wiping the residue of saliva and blood from his mouth. Pietro smile is instantly wiped away as he watches the girl run to

Syrus's aid, helping the boy sit up, gently caressing his injured face. "You stupid bitch," Pietro snarls at Annabeth. "You're still siding with him. He's a thing, a beast!"

"The only beast I see is you, Pietro!" Annabeth snaps back, her eyes filled with pure rage. Her words carry more power than the punches Pietro through at Syrus. "The man I see here is Syrus. You are nothing but a disgusting pig," Annabeth seethes. Pietro is taking aback by her words, carelessly speaking her thoughts. No woman should talk to a man like that. She's a disgrace.

Pietro's fists shook with rage. He wanted to destroy the enemy right here and then but not without provoking Syrus. He's seen the real power the boy possesses, and that was when he struck Annabeth all those years ago. She is his strength, and Pietro needs to destroy it.

"I'll you leave two to your darkened paths. You both will get your due," Pietro hisses at them both before disappearing back into the forest.

Syrus remains silent. He watches the older male leave and taking shallow breaths. He feels the sharp sting with every intake of breath, his eyes water and his own head begins to pound. The skin on his face tightens swell. Syrus looks to Annabeth with blurry eyes, feeling the salty water escape as they weep. Annabeth purses her lips, fury flowing through her boded. She shakes and cries, her breath quickens, and she replays the situation that had unfolded in her head. She slaps Syrus's swollen face. He grimaces. The sting numbly touches but can still feel something. He takes the hit without contempt.

"That is for giving into his taunts and starting the fight!" she snarls, in between deep breathes. Tears stream from her eyes, flowing down her olive skin. "I could have lost you," she weeps. Syrus's heart breaks in two, his bruised hands slowly, shakily move to Annabeth's hand. Syrus gently holds her soft hand in his, she clings onto it.

"I know," Syrus croaks. "I'm sorry for scaring you," he whispers to her. Using his spare hand, and gently caresses her face, his thumb wiping away the tears. Annabeth holds onto his hands, leaning into Syrus's touch, moving closer and closing her eyes, focusing on his warm touch, calming herself down in the process. Annabeth's heart slows, her breathing becomes levelled, her rage soothes and quells. Her tears slow, the lump in her throat goes. Slowly she opens her emerald eyes. They're brighter and glossier from her tears.

Both are uncaring how close her and Syrus's faces are. Their noses are inches apart. They can feel the warmth from their breaths, lips almost ghosting one another, so close, yet so far away. Syrus wants to give in and move nearer, but is this right? Should he do this, should he steal her kiss, is it wrong? Is any of this wrong, but why does he want to make it all right?

Annabeth is the one to make a move, sealing their lips together, so warm, gentle, and soft. Syrus's heart soars, all reason leaves as he focuses on the feeling of their lips together, the love he holds for Annabeth only blossoms. She slowly breaks away, their foreheads only touching now, both smiling like idiots as they stay in each other embrace.

"Won't your father kill me for me?" Syrus chuckles.

"What my father doesn't know won't hurt him," She whispers, her breath gently fanning Syrus's face.

"So, what is this kiss for?" Syrus teases her. Annabeth smiles and leans in again, their touching yet again for a quick peck.

"For what you said earlier," Annabeth answers and kisses him again and again before they had to pull back for air.

"Marry me?" Syrus blurts out, only to regret his words the second he uttered them. Annabeth only smiles, her thumb gently caressing his bruised skin.

"When we're both ready," she whispers. "But I am yours, just as you are mine."

Syrus swore he could cry right here and then if he wanted to, overjoyed to hear those words, thankful he has her in his life, filling Syrus with so much hope, abling him to push on, to prove those who have done him wrong. He is no beast, no creature of the undead. Syrus is a human, who happened to be born at the wrong time, but it does not mean he is cursed.

Syrus can finally say he is happy with his life.

9th of Janus

Syrus has reached adulthood, thanks to Alenxadros's efforts, of course. Much to his bragging, he never holds it against Syrus but is proud to keep a child alive and raise it till it is old enough to look after itself. Alenxandros's lover would have been proud of him.

As Saturnalia has finished and the new month of Janus has dawned upon them, Alenxadnros's excitement is nearly uncontained as he eagerly prepares a small celebration for his adoptive son. He knows he has all the time in the world since Syrus is hunched over his desk, light snores coming from the sleeping man. Alexandros quietly tip-toes over, finding papers are scattered all over his desk, drawings of the battlefield, with critical points of technical maneuvers in the upcoming battle. Alexandros remembers when Syrus's strategies have been put to use for the first time, speaking out in the war chamber, damming the older men as they were willing to put so many lives on the line. Syrus's quick thinking had lead them to the path of victory that day. He was only seventeen at the time. Alexandros could have not been prouder when he was told the news.

Alexandros smiles to himself and sneaks out of Syrus's room, gently closeing the door. He usually would wake the boy up, no matter how late he was working, but today he can make an exception for this is a special day.

Alexandros grabs a woollen shawl draping it over his aging body. His muscles have toned down, his skin has paled as he stays away from the sun, wrinkles have appeared on his hands, his eyes, and lips. His hands are more boney than they used to be, his hair has greyed, no longer the luscious black locks they once were, the hair on his arms and legs have thinned. Alexandros's back has also given way over the years, aching whenever he tends to the crops.

Alexandros opens the wooden door to the outside world with a wry smile. The cold wind gusts into the warm house, howling through the corridors. Alexandros holds the shawl closer to his body, cursing the wind. Winter has been harsher this year than usual. He wonders if their celebrations to the sun god had been enough for the upcoming spring. Has it strengthen him, or will they fall into a deep winter?

Arriving closer to the gates, Alexandros can see the young woman waiting for him. Almost the same height as Alexandro, she brings the older man into a hug. Knowing him for so long, Alexandros is practically family by this point.

Her hair has grown longer since she was sixteen, ensuring it is messily tied up into a bun, keeping it out from her face. She is Her body is slender, olive skin beautiful, and clear from any complections. Her hand is highly sought out by many male suitors, but she has turned them all down, just as her father did. Annabeth's father has always wanted her to have the best and with Syrus's contribution to the army and his intellect. He has proven his worth to the man. Perfect for his Daughter, and he does not want it any other way.

"Is your father aware of your disappearance?" Alexandros chuckles as they slowly walk to the morning markets. Annabeth laughs in response.

"He is aware, and he gives his regards to you and Syrus as well," She giggles. Annabeth couldn't contain her excitement. "Speaking of, where is the birthday boy?" she enquires with a broad smile, showing off her white teeth.

"Hunched over his desk asleep," Alexandros snickers. Annabeth giggles in response. Already she can picture her love asleep. He will undoubtedly complain about how sore he will be when he wakes up.

"Now, we need food, several candles, wine," Annabeth begins to list, and Alexandros just nods his head in silence. Happily agreeing with every demand the young woman makes, he can see how much she wanted to make this celebration special. In her eyes, too many birthdays have gone uncelebrated due to Syrus's distaste for them. He still blames himself in some way for all those who died so long ago. In the back of his head, Syrus believes his birth is a curse. His existence is a curse. Hence why he does not wish to celebrate his birthday. "Alexandros?" Annabeth had snapped him from his thoughts, his dull brown eyes look to her. "Is something the matter?' she asks the older gentleman. Alexandros only shrugs her concern off. Dismissing his own worry, all in the name to keep her content.

"It is nothing to worry about," he assures her and gives the young lady a warm smile. She sighs but lets it go, knowing there is more to this but remains quiet for now.

"Very well. I shall go get the fruits. May you get some wine?" Annabeth asks of Alexandros. He nods and watches the young lady walk away.

Alexandros took his time and delve back into his inner thoughts. Syrus has expressed these concerns with Alexandros, researching as much as he can about the vampyr king, even going into the royal library to learn from past scholars, writing letters, and sought information outside of the Roman borders but in his quest, he has been given nothing but a deadline. All vampyr kings turn at the age of twenty-one. Syrus was in tears when he learned of this news. As much as he denies it, fights it, there is a niggling voice, cruelly laughing at him. Telling Syrus he is a monster, and he should be hated and blamed for everyone's misfortune and loss all those years ago. Alexandros had to soothe the boy assuring him they are all still wrong. No one can predict the next king, it is impossible, and the warlock (remarkably and annoyingly still alive) is false, and Syrus will prove that today.

***

Syrus groans as he slowly moves his stiff body, feeling his muscles ache and his neck hurt as he tries to move it. Why did his body think it was a good idea to sleep on the desk? He groans once more and straightens himself up from the wooden desk, hearing his bones crack and his muscles ache around his spine. *Ugh, I'm getting old.* Syrus thinks to himself, getting up from his chair.

Looking back to his desk, Syrus looks over the papers skew all over the place. He notices smudged ink on one of the documents, peculiarly where his face was. Syrus's slowly lifts his hand to his face, carefully caressing his cheek, feeling the wet, sticky texture on his skin. Heaving a deep sigh, he meticulously grabs a random cloth from the floor, uncaring how long it has been down there. It will all get washed in the end. Stumbling over to the mirror and desperately tries to rid of the black ink on his face.

Syrus stares back at his reflection, growing ever more frustrated as he watches the ink smudges further down his neck. He's just thankful it hadn't gotten into his hair – no scratch that it did. His hair had grown out a bit longer than he was at sixteen. Loosely hanging around his ears, the tips just reaching past his jaw bone, it is just long enough for Syrus to tie back in a minor plat. It's a shame some of it is dipped in ink. His physique has stayed the same, shoulders a little broader, still lanky but taller than he once was, and even able to put up a fight when necessary. Many of his rivals have gone to the battlefield, and the rest have left Syrus alone. They all understand his importance to the general and to the success of the empire.

He hears the front door creak open and stops what he is doing. The light stomping of footsteps came thundering in soon after.

"Syrus?" he hears Alexandros call out.

"I'm in here," he responds and pays his attention back to the mirror, furiously rubbing his ink-stained face. Syrus does not mind the pair of footsteps coming to the door, thinking it is Alexandros but stops when he hears the light giggle. Syrus freezes, slowly turning his head away from the mirror, his heart leaping from his chest, plummeting down to his stomach.

Annabeth laughs at the taller male, sauntering over hands held behind her back, a grin formed by her light pink lips.

"My, my, my, what have you done to yourself?" she muses, gently grabbing the cloth from his hand.

"Would you believe I had to battle a dangerous ink monster?" Syrus jokes, just to hear her laugh. Her emerald eyes shift over to the desk, noticing the large ink puddle on Syrus's desk.

"And fought this beastly creature away, didn't you?" she rolls with it, walking over to the bowl of water next to Syrus's bed. Syrus follows like a lost lamb, always wanting to be near his beloved. He wants to touch her, hold her, and kiss her.

"Valiantly, the beast never stood a chance," Syrus stands tall, his chest slightly puffing out. Annabeth smiles at her love stringing the cloth of the loose drops of water. Straightening her back, her own chest touches Syrus's gently brushing against each other, her wet hands gently caress his cheek and the cold, damp cloth rubbing against his skin.

"Thankfully, you only got away with a stain," She whispers, inching her face closer to his.

"I'm fortunate," Syrus whispers, his face inching closer till their lips meet.

The kiss, however, was cut short due to an elderly gentleman clearing his throat, both adults pulling away, looking down at their feet, both feeling like children once more when they were caught in Alexandros's room taking his swords from the display.

"Happy birthday, my boy," Syrus's hazel eyes stare into the old man's brown ones, fear creeping up his spine. He had forgotten today was the big day. Syrus saw Alexandros's hug coming and still welcomed the embrace with a final pat on his back. Syrus thought back to when he woke this morning, and it had been the same as every other morning. Still feeling sore and very much human. He doesn't feel a need or urge to drink blood, he didn't see fangs, he didn't have red eyes or slit pupils. He hasn't noticed any changes. He still feels his own heartbeat profoundly within his chest. Syrus even takes a deep breath, realising his own body is begging for air.

Alexandros lets go of the boy. Both his and Syrus's stomachs growl loudly together, signalling their hunger. Both bursting into laughter. Leading both him and Annabeth out of the room, a small banquet is laid out before his eyes to the living area. A mix of seasonal fruits, honey, slices of bread and a bottle of excellent wine to go with.

"Thank you," Syrus whispers, feeling a surge of happiness soar within his chest.

"Happy birthday, my love," Annabeth whispers to him, holding onto Syrus's hand, their fingers entwining together. *Happy birthday to me.*

Dishonourable Soldier

Syrus expected to spend the rest of his birthday working. He did not anticipate a small celebration to occur on behalf of Annabeth's father, nor would he believed to be personally invited back to the General's house with Annabeth and Alexandros by his side. For Syrus, it was an unusual experience to be surrounded by familiar faces who have been friendly to him in the last three years. Their opinions of Syrus slowly changed, no longer believing the stories and rumours they have heard amongst society.

Syrus naturally felt uncomfortable. He's never been part of any social function in his life, even kindness and human decency from those he does not know all too well. It's almost sad really, there's a dark niggling thought lurking in the back of his head, whispering, murmuring half-truths. *'They only like you for your mind of war. They will turn their backs on you. You are still not trusted by them.*

Annabeth has taken notice of Syrus's withdrawn. He is more reserved to those who wish him a happy birthday or congratulating him for his past victories. He especially ignores the praise to Annabeth's father for taking Syrus under his wing and saving the boys social status. The last one is a bit backhanded, but Syrus barely acknowledges them before quickly dismissing himself and hiding away within the garden.

Annabeth, of course, is quick to follow her love. Concern fills her as she watches him inhales deep breaths. She gently holds onto his shoulder. Syrus accepts the warm hand as he feels his body shake. Annabeth soothes her lover, gently rubbing Syrus's back, giving him words of encouragement.

Syrus remembers to focus on the small sounds around him in the garden, something Alexandros taught him when he had to meditate. The leaves rustling in the wind, Syus's skin prickles with goosebumps from the cold, small birds sing in the distance, the smell of fresh mildew on the shaded grass.

"I'm ok," Syrus breathes. "Just too many people," he whispers. Annabeth understood, Syrus has ever only socialized with two people in his life and slowly has gotten used to her Father. He has only seen the worse from humanity. The only small glimpse of kindness came from her and Alexandros. So many people at once in a room where they could lash out on him at any moment sickened Syrus. Fear could only riddle his body as the dark thoughts slip into the forefront of his head. "I don't mean to ruin the party," he breathes.

"You haven't. Take your time," Annabeth soothes, rubbing his back.

"You don't have to wait with me," Syrus breathes out a short laugh but continues to focus on the sounds around him.

"I'm not leaving if my love is in distress. I will stay by your side," Annabeth whispers and continues to rub his back

"Syrus?" Syrus's eyes snap open, his head turning back, looking past his beloved to find her father standing before them.

The years have not been kind to him. His hair has greyed and thinned out, his eyes always look tired and worn, the cruel demeanour has washed away as he aged, but instead, he has only become tired of it all. His memory is not like what it used to be. Syrus had to gently remind the general what they had discussed the night before, regularly he would storm into Syrus's chambers, blaming the others for changing the posts on the map, but yet it was Syrus and him who made those changes. The general no longer saw Syrus as a threat but as an associate and one he could trust.

"Sir, I do apologize, I -." Syrus was merely cut off by the general's hand.

"Annabeth can you, please excuse us? I wish to talk to Syrus – alone," Annabeth's father adds, knowing full well his daughter would stay unless specified. Annabeth's hand wonders to Syrus's side, squeezing his own hand for reassurance before letting go and passing her Father before warning him. "Be kind to him."

The two men are left alone. The General straightens his back, humming shortly after.

"You've impressed me, boy," The general begins. "When I first enlisted you to train under my wing, I had hoped the stories were true," Annabeth's father wonders closer to Syrus. "I thought if we had a monster in our ranks, our enemies would fear us," he mutters before falling into a coughing fit. Syrus wasn't surprised to hear this. He had a suspicion when he first defeated the General in a game. Syrus is never easily fooled. His intelligence scared those who visit the boy under the General's eye.

"I knew it was your intention. I'm sorry to disappoint you," Syrus smiles, teasing the older man but concerned about his health. The General waves his hand, taking gulps of air and levelling his breath once more.

"It's okay. I realised they were wrong a long time ago," The father responds after taking another gulp of air. "I only kept you around for your talent of war, but then I watched you and Annabeth . . ." he trails off, his old eyes looking back inside. Annabeth talking to the other guests, Syrus could only marvel at her from afar, never growing tired of her smile, her green eyes glimmering in the sunlight. "I want you to marry my daughter." Syrus's heart leapt from his chest as he hears these words, his mouth goes dry, and his hands begin to shake.

"Marry?" Syrus's voice croaks. Annabeth's father glares at the young man, misjudging Syrus's shock.

"Is that a problem?" he growls. Syrus snaps out of his fear, quickly sucking in the air and calming himself.

"No," Syrus shakes his head. "I was taken by surprise. I never thought you would insist that I would take her hand. I thought you had in mind for someone else," Syrus remains calm, a small smile appearing on the corners of his mouth. The general eases and breathes.

"I did when she was young, a union was to be made between her and another man, but you came along and took her heart. She is the only thing I have left of her mother. I want her to be happy," he whispers.

"I . . . don't know what to say," Syrus murmurs, his eyes falling back to Annabeth.

"Nothing, I've already had the date planned, and you will take her hand," he laughs. "There's nothing else for you to say other show up and say I do," he laughs louder and slaps Syrus on the back of the shoulder. Syrus smiles, chuckling with the General as giddy excitement overwhelms him.

Both men walk back inside, still laughing, with broad grins on their faces, but they both fall as they take note of the room's atmosphere. Annabeth is quick to be by Syrus's side, her hands clinging to his arm. Many of Syrus's associates whisper amongst each other, all parting away from the unannounced intruder.

'What is he doing here?'

'I heard they discharged him for not following orders.'

'I thought he killed one of our own?'

"Petro," The General snarls at Syrus's older brother. "What are you doing in my home?" Annabeth's father demands. Pietro was quick to fall on his knees, bowing before the General.

"I have come to apologize for my behaviour on the battlefield," Pietro begins. Annabeth's father's hand tighten in their grasp, his scowl sours, eyes filled with fury. "I wish to ask for your forgiveness and give me a second chance," Pietro remains monotonous. Not a hint of regret is laced within his voice.

"Get out," the General snarls. "You come in here asking for forgiveness after what you have done. You are a disgrace to the people of Rome!" he shouts at Pietro.

"You may think I am a disgrace, but not when you bring that thing into your home," Pietro snarls, pointing directly to Syrus. Syrus only sighs and rolls his eyes, tired of the accusations against him since the warlock and his false prediction. "Accepting it as one of us," Pietro snarls. "I refuse to follow the orders of a traitor!" Pietro stands on his feet, his eyes trained on Syrus.

"A traitor? A traitor!? You abandoned your post, left men to die, and for what? Because your pride demanded it so!" The General's voice booms within the house, his screams reach to the outside.

The guards of Rome come rushing in through the front door. Questions flew from their mouths, asking if their beloved General is all right. "Get this thing out of my home," he commands his guards. Pietro threw the guards off him. They desperately try to remove the unwanted guest.

"You will get what's coming to you, monster," Pietro hisses and finally – willingly leaves. Everyone is left in stunned silence. All eyes land on Syrus and Annabeth clinging to his arm. As much as he does not want to admit it, there is dread pooling deep within Syrus's stomach, knowing Pietro will keep true to his promise.

Growing pains

Syrus lets his brother's words sink back to the deepest parts of his mind, not wanting to put any energy into his brother. Focus on the present and look to the future. Syrus has proven himself that he is not the so-called beast as they all claimed him to be.

News of their union travelled quickly amongst the people. Annabeth already had her suspicions. She is not so easily fooled as her father is led to believe. Alexandros isn't surprised. He only grins and mutter the words, 'about time,' to Syrus and kept on reading, with wine by his side.

Although Syrus is excited for their union to be official, he has not had time to speak with Annabeth or the celebrated day. All he knows is the date and what to say on that day. Twenty third of Janus is the wedding day, preparations are already made, servants are pushed to grab necessary items for the day, plan the invites, and order food. All of this rushing is hurting his head. As if the end is near, and they must prepare for the close of humanity.

Syrus smiles to himself and continues to plan out for future battles. In his spare time, he does this research through old war stories, learning from the great battles Rome has fought and diving into other countries' war stories.

"Syrus!" he hears Alexandros's cry from the other room.

"Yes!" he answers back, his nose still stuck in a book, messily scribbling down notes.

"Have you eaten yet? I made you breakfast, and you haven't touched it!" Alexandros yells, the apparent hint of annoyance in his voice. Syrus stops and thinks for a moment, he knows he hasn't eaten anything, but he hasn't had an appetite since his birthday. His work could be getting in the way, so focused on strategy food has slipped his mind. This is an unhealthy habit to get into. Syrus better remind himself to eat more.

"Uh, no. Sorry," Syrus put his pen down and hastily walks into the same room, Alexandros crossing his arms, the bowl of watered oats sitting on the table since this morning. Syrus shrinks under the older man's gaze. He may be a man now, but he is not too old to be disciplined. "I've been busy with work. I haven't been hungry," Syrus sheepishly explains, grabbing the bowl and taking it outside, scrapping the scraps into the wild. Alexandros pops his head from the door, still sour over wasted food but sighs and brushes it away. He will let this pass, just this once. "Fine, I have made you dinner. You can at least sit down and enjoy a meal with your old man," he gruffs.

"I'll humour you," Syrus teases, coming back inside.

Both men sit at the table, already Alexandros has made work on his meal, but Syrus seemed reluctant. He's not hungry like he usually is. Even putting a piece into his mouth, it doesn't taste the same as he once remembered. Something is off. Why isn't he enjoying the food? It's bland, tasteless. The texture didn't feel right on his tongue either. He struggled to swallow the food down, feeling it slowly slide down his throat and hitting his stomach, churning in protest as the food is dissolved in the acids.

"My cooking can't be that bad?" Alexandros laughs it off, trying to not sound worried, but he can't help but notice Syrus's pale face.

"No, no. It's fine," Syrus finally spits out, carefully trying to pick his words while still feeling his stomach roll. "I could be coming down this something or maybe nervous wedding jitter," Syrus shrugs it off and gently pushes his meal away. "I mean, it is a big deal," Syrus sighs. Alexandros straightens himself and nods.

"It is a commitment you both take together," Alexandros smiles.

"Did you ever marry your partner?" Syrus asks, and Alexandros's smile saddens.

"No, he was never one for marriage. My presence was more than enough to prove our union," he chuckles.

"You never spoke about him much," Syrus whispers, feeling his own heartache, reflecting the loss Alexandros went through. It's almost unbearable if he lost Annabeth. She kept him from drowning in the dark.

"I didn't," Alexandros agrees. "But I should have .. . spoken about him. I did his memory no justice," Alexandros rasps.

"How . . . did he die?" It is a sensitive question, one Syrus has always wanted to ask, but it is only now that he has the courage.

"A vampyr," Alexandros simply responds, his demeanour going a little cold. "We were hunting it in the northern borders of the empire. This one was smart and ambushed us, I was in direct line of its attack, but he pushed me out of the way and . . ." Alexandros cuts himself off, swallowing loudly, his eyes begin to water. "His throat torn apart as the beast feasted upon his blood. I reacted as quickly as possible but, I was too late. No matter how hard I tried to stop the bleeding, I couldn't. He died in my arms that night. His last words were, I love you," Alexandros's voice dulls to a whisper, his old eyes stare deep into his plate as if they held the answers to his pain. A small tear leaked from his eye, slowly sliding down his cheek.

"I'm sorry," Syrus whispers, grabbing the man's hand, giving it a tight squeeze.

"It's all right, I should talk about him more," Alexandros gives a weak smile, patting Syrus's hand, and let's go. "Now, get some rest. We can't have you sick leading up to your big day," Alexandros ushers the young man to bed. He could only nod and not ignore his reasoning, finding himself move his feet to his dark room.

Finding comfort in the dark. Maybe a good night's rest will ease Syrus's symptoms.

***

Although they are through the middle of winter, Syrus can't seem to shake the heat away from the sun's rays. While others felt the cold and welcomed the warmth, Syrus could only swelter in the heat, avoiding the harsh sun and cool off in the shade. Everything is just so bright. His eyes can't even handle the light anymore. This isn't good, he has to be in good health for the wedding. He has even begun to feel weak, drained even and has the constant urge to sleep, constantly snapping out of the tempting slumber at the last minute.

"You're off," Alexandros snaps, quickly knocking Syrus off his feet and placing the tip of his iron sword on his chest. "You feeling ok? If you fought any enemy in this condition, you would die," he huffs, removing his weapon from Syrus's chest and gives his hand. Taking Alexandros's hand and breathing heavily, he felt like collapsing to the ground again. His legs shake as he tries to stabilize himself on his own two feet. The heat from the sun is getting a little too much. He can barely open his eyes.

"Sorry, I'm just really not feeling well," Syrus huffs, even talking take it out of him. Alexandros hums, putting his hand against the young man's forehead.

"You're burning up. You must have caught something," The older man grumbles, sheathing his sword. "You should have said something," disappointment lacing his voice, and he stares Syrus down. Feeling like a child once more, Syrus bows his head.

"I didn't want anyone to worry. I didn't want people to think," Syrus cuts himself off. Any sign of weakness and this city will surely eat him alive.

"You proved them wrong. You are just sick. Any human can catch a cold," he assures his son, gently guiding Syrus back to the house. "It's expected in this weather. Go get some rest, and don't come out till your feeling better," he orders. Gently pushing Syrus into his room and closing the door behind Syrus.

Heaving a final sigh, he takes his father's advice and slowly slumps himself into bed, exhausting washes over Syrus as soon as his head hits the pillow.

Promises to keep

It is a week before the wedding, and Syrus's health has turned for the better, slowly he feels to be regaining his strength, able to stay awake more and keep some food down, but everything is still tasteless and bland, much to his stomach's displeasure he always pushes through and eats.

Alexandros hasn't pushed him as much lately, keeping an eye on his health, making sure Syrus is ok. He asks every ten minutes – well, not literally, but Syrus has counted up to twenty times a day. Tiring as it is but thankful, he has someone watching out for him.

Annabeth, of course, started to dote on him since word reaches her home. She dropped everything to take care of Syrus's health. He never liked to be fussed over, even as a child.

"Now, are you sure you will be all right?' Annabeth asks again. Keeping count, this would be the fifth time tonight.

"I'm sure I am fine. We are just going to have a nice dinner with your father," Syrus assures her. Something else Syrus has taken note of is how he feels stronger with Annabeth around.

"Hmm," she begins, slanting her eyes and intensely stare upon his more than usual pale face. "Fine," she huffs and pays attention to the path in front of her. They both walk in silence before Annabeth pipes up once more. "If my Father mentions anything about children, please say we are waiting."

"Children?" Syrus smiles, amused at how this topic suddenly came about.

"He's been praying to the gods for a grandson, and I tell him the gods might want a granddaughter instead, and besides we need a home suitable for them," Annabeth begins her rant, something she has wanted to discuss with Syrus for some time. "Your home is much too small, and Father will just pester us," she angrily sighs. "As well as trying to make do all these silly rituals for us to have a boy." Syrus gently grasps his love's hand. She stops and looks at Syrus's loving eyes.

"Boy or girl, I will love them dearly," Annabeth relaxes.

"Truly? You wouldn't want a son just so they can carry the family name," she quips.

"I don't care. I would be over the moon if we had a child, boy, or girl, as long as they are happy and healthy," Syrus assures her, gently kissing the top of her hand. Annabeth embraces her love, happy to hear such sweet words come from his mouth.

"You have come so far," she whispers. "You stay standing no matter what the gods throw at you. I am so proud," Syrus wraps his arms around her petite body, sighing against her shoulder, thankful to have her in life. He smiles at the idea of children. It made his heart soar, having little ones of their own, a family, a place to call home.

"Isn't this sweet?" the same familiar, chilling voice creeps from the darkness. Dread travels through Syrus's spine. He quickly spins around, shielding Annabeth from any harm. He could feel a growl resonating within his chest, something primal awakening within. He can feel it, subtle but waiting till it is the right time to come out. More than five men came out from the dark shadows of the dirt street, Pietro leading them all out from the pits of darkness. Some held big wooden clubs, other carried iron swords, and one holding a mace. Syrus's heartbeat erratically as fear spikes into his blood, eyes snapping to every enemy that dared to come closer. They were, unfortunately, surrounded. "And here I thought I had to meet you at the General's house," Pietro grins.

Syrus was too slow to react, wishing he had eyes in the back of his head as Annabeth was pulled from his protective grip. Desperately he tries to fight back but is also held down by two other men by the arms. Syrus thrusts his weight around, hoping to lessen the men's grip but cannot shake them off, and he is pushed down to the ground. Syrus is still weak, slowly recovering from whatever illness he came down with.

"Let her go!" Syrus snarls, staring Pietro down, pleading on the inside that he listens. One of the men holding Syrus down knocks him on the head. Black spots appear in his vision, feeling his skull pound.

"No can do, little brother," he snickers, raising his own iron sword to Syrus's throat. "I have been dreaming of this moment for some time," Pietro grins. "You may have everyone else fooled but not us. We see you for what you really are," he hisses, slowly dragging the edge of the blade across Syrus's neck. He can feel the slight warmth of his own blood trickle down his skin.

"Don't touch him!" Annabeth screams, thrashing about in her own captor's hands. Pietro angrily sighs and pulls back the blade.

"Ah yes, Annabeth. I almost forgot about you," Pietro saunters over, his own hand gently gliding over her face. She desperately tries to move away from his touch. "No one ever dared to correct you because you're the general's daughter." Pietro strikes Annabeth, her head snapping to the left, feeling her cheek throb. She winces but does not cry, refusing to give him any satisfaction. Syrus saw red, fighting against the men thrashing about, screaming obscenities, but he was useless, weak, and human. "A woman like you should know their place. Always speaking out as if you were a man, it's disgusting," Annabeth glowers at Pietro, spitting in his face in defiance. Out of rage, he strikes again, but this time she was unflinching. Her eyes held a fire within them as she stares down her captive.

"Futuo," she hisses, and Pietro raises his hand once before Syruse cuts in.

"Enough! Please, just stop." Pietro lowers his hand, looking over his shoulder, and smile back at Syrus. "It's between you and me. Just let her go, please!" Pietro just snorts at Syrus's pleas and stares back into Annabeth's fiery eyes.

"You're a fool," Pietro whispers, turning back to Syrus once more and drawing the sword to his throat once more. "Looks like I'll be killing you first."

"Kill me and let him go. He doesn't deserve any of this." Everyone freezes into place as Annabeth screams those words. Syrus's heart sank as he stares at her with pleading eyes. Pietro lowers his weapon and sniggers before kneeling down to Syrus's eyes. He loved seeing the look of fear and dread contorting on Syrus's face, and Pietro knew how to make the blow even more damaging.

"Looks like you committed another soul to die for you. Remember that night, Syrus, how our parents fought for your cursed existence, how they sacrificed themselves for you to live," Pietro berates, his jaw tightening, remembering the night so vividly himself. The anguish cries and screams filling the dark void of the night, the smell of iron from the blood spilled, the burning heat from the fires set alight to the pile of bodies on the street. "So many souls died that night. You should have been one of them," Pietro hisses.

"They would have done the same for you," Syrus bites out, his body shaking, dread overcoming him.

"No, they wouldn't," Pietro stand back up, stalking again over to Annabeth. "I thought about killing you both, but I wonder, which is more painful?" Before anyone had the chance to answer, Pietro thrust his iron blade into Annabeth's torso. Her eyes widen from the jolting pain she felt as it punctures her stomach. Blood begins to gush out like a geyser. Syrus watches from afar, unable to do anything as he watches the love of his life dying before him. Her shining green eyes lose their sparkle, her olive skin bruised from Pietro's blows. She coughs up blood, watching it pool out from her mouth, staining her white teeth.

Pietro let her go. They all watch her crumple to the ground, laughing as she is dying in a pool of her own blood. Pietro waves his hand to his men and lets go of Syrus.

Rushing to her side, panic flooding his brain, desperately using his hand to slow the bleeding, the warm sticky blood coating his fingers, he lifts her head up, his entire body is shaking, salty tears leak from his eyes as he watches her give him one last smile.

"You're going to be ok, please don't go, please," Syrus cries desperately, unable to stop shaking. With the last ounce of her strength, Annabeth lifts her hand and gently holds his cheek.

"Stay strong, my love," she rasps, blood leaking from her lips. "I love you."

Those were the last words she spoke before her hand collapses to the cold hard ground. Syrus felt like all the air had been sucked out of his lungs. His chest ached like it was pierced. The sharp stab going through his heart, heavy and painful. His shaking is uncontrollable at this point, and his tears flow like a never-ending waterfall. Sobs wracking through his whole body and hold her lifeless corpse close to him. Begging the gods, some unforsaken being to bring her back, give her life back and take him instead.

"To kill one and let the other live. I think this is a fitting punishment for you, baby brother," Pietro grabs Syrus's hair from the back, pulling his lips close to Syrus's ear. "Your existence brings nothing but death to those who come into contact with you. This death is all on you," he whispers and throws Syrus down onto Annabeth's body.

As much as he tried to ignore the dark whispers in his head, the evil dark thoughts they murmured to him since he was a child.

'you bring nothing but death and misery.'
'They all hate you.'
'She died because of you.'

They're right. Syrus thinks. Mourning over his love, holding her body close to his. *She died because of me. My parents sacrificed themselves for me. So many are dead, and yet I live. I'm not a monster. I'm not! I'm human. I've always been human. Please . . . someone . . . end my existence.*

The horrible Truth

Today is the twenty-third of Janus. Instead of a union between two people, it became a funeral. The day is insultingly sunny, the wind gently blows, birds singing a bouncy tune, all unbeknownst that today is meant to be a miserable day.

To Syrus, everything is bleak and dull. Even if the sun shines brightly, it's dark and dim. Holed up in his room, barring himself against the door, blankly staring at the stone floor, uninterested in moving, in eating, he couldn't even sleep. His dreams are only plagued with nightmares. Watching Annabeth die over and over in his head or find her decayed corpse in her sarcophagus and her eyes snapping open, grasping onto Syrus's throat, letting out a shrilling scream from the dislocated jaw, skin, and flesh melting off her skull, eyes melting. Syrus could only watch in horror before jolting himself awake from his slumber.

"It's not your fault, you know," Syrus hears Alexandros through the door. For the last week, he has tried to coax Syrus out of his room, trying to get him to eat, talk, and grieve with a loved one, but of course, Syrus chooses to suffer alone. "He shouldn't have blamed you. You were outnumbered."

"I promised," Syrus croaks. Finally, using his voice, ragged and hoarse from underuse in the last week. "I promised I would protect her," he whispers, feeling his chest ache. "And he trusted me to look after his daughter."

Syrus reflects on the night he carried Annabeth's body back to her father, the begging, the pleading. He knew Syrus had no hand in her death, but he was angry. He entrusted Syrus with his daughter, ensured she would always be safe with him, but instead, it was her undoing.

'I never want to see your face again.' Those words still echo in Syrus's head, cruelly reminding him he cannot attend the funeral and mourn. There is no closure for him.

"It's still not your fault," Alexandros simply replies. Syrus only shakes his head, frustration growing in his core. Alexandros waits for Syrus to respond but understands he will not get an answer. "It gets easier," Alexandros continues. "No matter how much you want to join them, you find another reason to go on."

To go on, huh. Syrus remains silent. *Is there a purpose for me to go on? What do I have left? Once Alexandros is gone, who else will be there?*

'Your existence brings nothing but death to those who come into contact with you.' *He's right; I bring nothing but death.* Syrus thinks

Syrus curls himself up into a ball, letting the ache in his chest consume him, tears spilling from his eyes. He no longer holds back his tears. Alexandros can only sit at the door and listen to the boy. Feeling helpless hearing his son cry alone. He wants to hug the boy like he did when he was a child, soothing his pain and worries. But this time, he wants to be alone.

Syrus decides to move away from the door and move over to his bed. Getting on his feet, he only begins to take one step. The ache in his chest noticeably started to burn, painfully spreading through Syrus's nerves, spreading to his fingertips, travelling down his spine, to his legs. Syrus sharply gasps, trying to ignore the pain. He keeps inhaling, feeling like his lungs are filled with fluid like he is drowning in water. He collapses to the ground, unable to stop his fall, hitting the stone floor with a hard thud. The only pain he feels is the excruciating burn through his body

It burns. Why – why won't it stop. Please make it stop. Everything inside – all of it – burning. As if the gods have set my insides alight. Nothing I do can stop the burning. Please, someone, anyone.

Syrus cries out, feeling the painful ache in his mouth like someone has broken his skull and forcing teeth deeper within the bone. Every intake of breath is nothing but agony. Knives are relentlessly stabbing into his lungs. His heart beats at an alarming rate, unable to steady itself nor slow down. It overworks itself and burns with each pulse.

Fuck!

Syrus silently screams, his voice no longer working, his body failing, shutting down, the world around begins to blacken, unable to see anything.

"Syrus?! Syrus!" Alexandros's shouts sounded muffled and far away as if he was on top of the mountain, and it echoes down to the base as a whisper.

***

Fuck. Fuck, everything hurts, this feeling. Hungry, so hungry.

It was the first thought that came to Syrus as he finally regains consciousness.

He feels different. He can feel the hunger gnawing at his sanity, slowly eating away, eating him up on the inside. A desire to quench it no matter the costs. His lungs feel empty, hollow. Syrus breathes and feels like it is going nowhere, other than the hypnotic sweet scent that caught his interest.

His eyes snap open, expecting daylight to flood through the bedroom window, but instead, he awakes in the night. Syrus expected a candle to be lit, but no, he can see in the pitch black, every tiny detail in his room, he can see the small cracks in the farthest corner. Syrus remembers the ache he felt in his upper mouth, noticing how full his mouth feels. Gently he brushes his tongue against his teeth, feeling two sharp points.

Dread only pools into Syrus's stomach. He begins to shake, feeling sick, the sudden realization kicks in. *They were right.* This thought crushed him. Tears well up in his eyes, spilling down his face. *No, no, no, no, no, no, no, no.* Syrus chants in his head, begging for this to be some cruel dream, pleading with the gods that this is a cruel joke, wishing some higher being can hear his wishes and take this curse away. *I can't be a vampyr, I can't be the king, I can't, no, no, no, no, please no.* Syrus curls up into a ball, tears still spilling from his eyes. *Please let this be a dream. Annabeth, oh gods, they killed her because it should have been me. It should have always been me.*

"Syrus." opening his eyes once more, Syrus can still see the empty room. Not a soul in sight, but distinct drumming is heard. Trailing to the wooden door, he can listen to it, thumping rhythmically. It's almost hypnotic to Syrus. His mouth becomes dry, his fangs begin to ache, the hunger gnaws at him, and the smell – oh so sweet. "Are you finally awake?" the voice snaps him out of his daze, recognizing the familiar gruff. He opens his mouth, ready to answer back.

Instead, Syrus closes his mouth and gently removes himself from the bed – Alexandros must have put him there. Nearly falling back to the ground, Syrus stabilised himself before moving to the door and reaching for the handle. Grasping the cold metal, he crushes it within his grasps. With a gentle twist, he was able to pull the door off its hinges. Syrus can only drop the wooden in defeat and let it fall to the stone ground. Alexandros stood on the other side of the room. Syrus does everything in his power to ignore the intoxicating scent, the heart banging into his skull, everything in his head, screaming to give in, to lunge, to feed.

"Well," Syrus rasps, struggling to speak with his elongated teeth. Alexandros clung to his sword, poised and ready if Syrus was to make a move. He is prepared to catch him off guard. Of course, this was all in the act of self-defence. "Deals, a deal. You said you would do it." Alexandros grits his teeth, reminding himself of the deal he made all those years ago.

Syrus, the cursed child, the one who should have died with the rest. Hundreds of lives were sacrificed, all meaningless because I saved him. Their deaths would have been noble. All of this is wrong. He didn't deserve the life the gods have given him. No one deserves such punishment. The world wanted to hate you just because you were born. "Alexandros," Syrus hisses, feeling the feral rage inside him bubbling to the surface. "kill me," he snarls, but Alexandros looks away, poising like a stone statue. "Look at me! They are right. I'm a monster, a beast!" Syrus feels the sharp sting on his fingertips. Looking down, he can see them forming into sharp claws, ready to slice open flesh. Snapping his attention back to his father, Alexandros drops the sword, shaking as tears flow from his eyes.

"I can't," he cries. "This city, this fucking city!" he shouts, banging his fist against the stone floor, uncaring about his sore hand. "If anyone is a monster, it's them," he cries, sobs wracking through his old body. "No one deserves a life you have lived. You didn't deserve any of it, regardless of the outcome." Syrus knew he is right. No one should have experienced the life he has lived. So many hated him, was it even necessary. He had become a monster just as they said he would, no matter how much Syrus denied it, fought against it, try to prove they were wrong . . . he became the very thing they predicted him to be. "You're not a monster," Alexandros snaps Syrus from his thoughts. His teary eyes bore into Syrus's. "You braved the masses, found love, you stood up for what was right. The only monsters I see are them." Syrus thinks back all these years, he only did this for one person and one person alone, and they took her from him. She was the only person that made his life bearable. His love, his only love. Would she have been better off if the change happened sooner? Would he have left this miserable city with her by his side, or would she reject like all the others? What then? Syrus knows he could never hurt her. Even if she hated him, he would just leave quietly. *But all that's changed.* Syrus thinks bitterly. If they genuinely believed he was a monster, Pietro would have killed him that night. He hoped Syrus would stay human.

"Maybe I should be a monster," Syrus murmurs, taking one step to the door.

"Don't do this, you go out, and you will prove everyone right, be better than them, Syrus. You can still prove them wrong!" Alexandros pleads. Syrus stands at the doorway. He was one step away from the outside world. One step from unleashing horrors upon the city. "If you step out that door, I will kill you," Alexandros gets back up on his feet, sword in hand. Syrus looks over his shoulder, giving Alexandros a smile one last time.

"I hope you do."

They wanted a Monster. I'll give them one.

Pietro tiredly walks into the tiny home he had acquired for himself since his dismissal. With no title or respect within the legion, he is an outcast amongst the nobles. It ate at him to be surrounded amongst the common rabble, but Pietro swears to himself, he will rise up again once words get out that he had finally slaughtered the cursed human. If he was truly meant to be a beast, Syrus would have become one ages ago.

The people looked for a scapegoat, and he was the perfect pawn. Pietro smiles to himself, remembering his adoptive father's words. *'That boy is a scapegoat, Pietro. The emperor wouldn't have allowed him to walk out of that building if he wasn't looking for another to take the people's hate.'* Pietro was angry back then, just as he is now. Watching his own parents give up their lives, they succeeded in their goal. They saved their beloved son but cursed the other.

Pietro punches the stone wall, frustration still bubbling beneath his chest. It doesn't matter anymore, Syrus will get his wish, and Pietro will be seen as a hero amongst the citizens of Rome. Annabeth's death was just to sweeten Syrus's agony.

Pietro closes the wooden door to his tiny home, tiredly moving his feet to his room, where his bed and small desk greets him, but something is off.

He takes one step into the room, and already a cold chill travels down his spine. His room feels colder as if death has come to visit him. His heart begins to beat louder, adrenaline kicking in, all signs point to run. Pietro took all his willpower and swallow the fear, scolding himself. Nothing is waiting for him in the dark.

"Hello, Pietro," the familiar voice calls to him within the darkness. It sounded so calm, pleasant, almost as if an old friend came to greet him once more. A spark is ignited, and a candle is lit from the corner of Pietro's room, the fire dances and only reveals half of the intruders face, the rest still masked in shadow, but Pietro knows who this intruder is, sitting on his chair.

"Syrus!" he snarls. The anger taking over his fear, ready to put up a fight against the weakling. "How did you get in here?!" Pietro demands, his fist clenched and ready to throw a punch. Syrus smiles, amused by his actions, tilting his head closer to the light. He noticed Pietro faltering, paling even, as fear slowly washes over the man once more.

"I don't know to be honest," Syrus begins, humming in amusement.

He thinks back to the moment he stepped out of the door from Alexandros's home. How calm Syrus felt to walk in the darkness, he no longer fears the shadows. The shadows fear him. To tread where the shadows of human life lie, the night bending his to his will.

The shocked gasps from the guard watching a shadow walk amongst their own in the stone walls. There is no one besides them to cast it in the dimly lit streets, and then the torches snuff out as Syrus passes.

He truly does not understand how this works, but it's useful, abling him to step into Pietro's home. "It's interesting like I can walk through shadows. It's an odd experience. I can't explain it myself, but it's certainly useful if I want to get into places where I am not welcomed," Syrus hisses, his clawed hand already grasping Pietro's throat. The human barely stood a chance. He didn't even see Syrus get up from the chair.

This is the true power of a vampyr. Pietro stares into Syrus's white eyes. He was so used to seeing his old hazel eyes, but instead, two terrifying black dots stare back at him.

Syrus is overwhelmed with the sweet scent filling his senses, the racing heartbeat so loud, his fangs ache, everything in him screaming to take the bite, and as much as Syrus wants to, he wants to draw this out as long as possible. Eliciting fear into Pietro's soul, making the little human beg as Syrus drains his life away.

Syrus throws Pietro to the ground, landing all his weight onto his elbow as he hits the ground. Pietro yelps, clinging onto his arm, wincing as he holds it close. Pietro remembers for a split second, reminding himself why he is in this position in the first place. His instincts to survive kick and punch. Syrus watches the human scrambling on the floor, desperately trying to reach for the door. Pietro's hand falters back, he begins to tremble on his knees as the sudden realization, he is no longer able to get to the exit. Syrus, already leaning against the door lazily, a dark, mischievous smile graces his lips. The sight is just too much.

Pietro body convulses as he begins to weep before the vampire. This is not what Pietro planned. This is not the death he had in mind. He pictured dying with loved ones surrounding him, all weeping over him in his final hours.

Syrus's eyes beeline for the blood weeping from Pietro's elbow. The hunger he has suppressed since his awakening flourished. His mind has begun to frenzy, no longer in control of his own actions, his fangs eagerly waiting to tear into soft flesh. Syrus lunges upon his prey, one clawed hand grasping its throat, the other lifting its injured arm. Syrus's dry tongue touches the sweet red nectar, all his nerves pulsate a pleasurable shock through his system as soon as he tasted the first drop. His brain is offline, and all there is the warm sweet blood, the pleasure, and the hunger begging to be sated. Syrus moves his tongue away from the cleanly licked wound, his nose seeking the best place to feed, uncaring to the prey's crying. Quite frankly, it's getting annoying. Moving his clawed hand away from his throat, Syrus wraps his hand around its mouth and begins to squeeze. Teeth and bone squish together like wet clay, ready to be shaped and moulded in Syrus's hand.

Muffled screams come from them, it didn't stop, but it is no longer loud as it was before. Tears start flowing, unable to cry and beg for freedom, its jaw has been crushed in. Syrus smiles at his handy work, not interested in the small streams leaking from its mouth. No, he was far more interested in its neck. He can hear the blood pump loudly, just underneath its skin. A growl resonates within Syrus's chest. He snarls before lunging down. Teeth tearing into flesh, reaching the vital artery. Satisfyingly pop into his mouth, and the warm flood fills into Syrus's mouth, smoothly sliding his throat as he desperately drinks. Uncaring of his strength, Syrus brings his pray closer, clawed hands grasping into the back of its head, digging into its skull. Bone, crushing under Syrus's grip, its shoulder shattered by the other clawed hand. It only releases a pained whine as everything begins to slow, feeling nothing but agony as its vision fades to black.

Syrus snarls and tears deeper into the flesh, desperate for more blood, frustrated that he is still unsatisfied. He needed more. Tearing his teeth from the dead tissue, he enjoys the lingering pleasure from his feed but then for it to be rudely interrupted by the firey blaze burning up within his body. It hurts, it all hurts, he needs more.

Standing up, he makes his way to the door, ready to inflict such misery upon the city, prepared to let the streets run red and then finally make it to the capital, where a nervous warlock waits for him.

Syrus's thoughts were put on hold as he hears a whisper in the darkness. He turns to the crumpled body, it has not moved, but something else is in the same room. Syrus watches in fascination, watching the clawed hand appear from the ground below. Its spindly arm pulls itself up from the ground. Its body lean and skeleton-like appearance, limbs jiggered and sharp, head round, like a person but with no face, only the darkness stares back at Syrus. Though on the other side of the room, Syrus can feel a cold breath near his ear, its dark whispers praising him, adoring him and pledging complete allegiance to him

"What . . . are you?" Syrus, unfortunately, is met with silence. "Can I . . . create more of you?" he asks instead, and the creature only nods his head. Syrus hums, thinking what he can do with these . . . things? He looks down at the body, thinking to himself how it's possible to create more, and the only way to be sure is to test it.

Sunset

Syrus happened to not be the only vampyr within this cursed city. As soon as the first drops of blood were spilled. All who were hiding in the shadows came out and revelled in the carnage.

Many guards fought valiantly, but they were too weak to go up against a mob of vampyrs. Desperate screams echo throughout the night, lasting to the early hours of the morning.

Blood is spilled upon the dirt ground, slowly tearing through the sectors of social hierarchy, starting from the poorest to the richest and then finally reaching the capital.

The vampyrs worship Syrus upon the ground he walks. It sickened him. So many have waited for this day, hoping the rumours were true. Their patience has been rewarded indeed, but it does not mean Syrus is what they expected. He has no desire in leading them. He doesn't care. The newly turned vampyr does not want this title. Syrus didn't care if they all died before him or create new vampyrs. All he cared about is his thirst for revenge.

He can feel his excitement grow as he takes each step closer up to the great hall. Where the emperor and the weak and feebled warlock remain. Many guards hold their ground at the entrance. Some charge at Syrus, running down the marble steps. A cruel glint in the vampyrs red eyes, his own hands sharpening to their dangerous talons, and within a blink of the guard's eyes, the creature disappears and reappears past them all, slowly making his way up the steps.

They all whither feeling excruciating pain within them, and one by one, the guards fall, blood spilling from the mouth, pooling from their abdomens. Many at the front line witness their comrades be slaughtered within a split second, and all make the wise decision to run.

Syrus steps echo within the large hall, screams are heard behind the large wooden doors. They argue and scream at each other, putting the blame on one another. A smile graces his lips, knowing who is behind those doors. But he would be disappointed if he misses killing them both before one kills the other.

"So, the mighty beast," Syrus focuses his attention on one man standing at the door, the only person between him and revenge. The old man sheathes his iron sword, his old and frail body tired from the carnage that is laid waste to the city. He knew about the small vampyr population, but he did not care to do anything since there was no immediate danger. "I wonder what Annabeth would say if she saw you like this," Syrus snaps. The general doesn't flinch as his face is close to Syrus's threatening gaze. He notes the long canines within his mouth, the terrifying snake pupils and the red eyes of the blood he has received from his victims.

The general grunts and takes a step back, unable to stand the iron stench coming from Syrus's breath. He could have died just then, but the old Syrus is in their still, and the old Syrus is grieving, taking it out on those who have hurt him. "She would still love you, I bet," Syrus's sanity snaps back into place. Memories of her sweet smile, her loving emerald eyes as she looks into his, he could still feel her warm touch on his cheek as she gently holds him. Syrus begins to tremble, tears spill from his eyes, his heartaches as if someone had torn a hole into his chest.

The General only sighs and pats him on the shoulder before moving away from his post. "I heard you killed Pietro first," without a word, Syrus nods, letting the tears fall. Annabeth's father smiles before looking at the wooden doors one last time. "Give them hell."

It was those final words that pushed Syrus back into his predatory stance, he didn't have to ask for permission, but the old man's words were enough to remind him why he started this in the first place.

The doors collapse of their hinges falling flat on the ground with a large crash, the wood splintering and splitting in two. The emperor and his pet warlock only shake in fear as they witness the monster they have inadvertently created.

Quick to react, the warlock casts a spell to summon a ball of fire, launching it at Syrus. The vampyr smirks, clicking his fingers, and a small group of shadows come up from the ground, taking the hit. They disperse and disappear into the darkness once again. They are not destroyed, just waiting to be called for once more.

The warlock stood in his place in disbelief, and Syrus took great pleasure in his shock.

"Do you like them?" he taunts the warlock, and two spindly shadows appear holding the warlock down in his place. "Something of my own odd creation. Always seeming to appear when I drain the living dry," Syrus stalks closer to his disabled prey.

The emperor cowardly makes a run for it, in the opposite direction. Syrus sighs tiredly, frustrated by the human's attempts to flee. The game of chase has certainly gotten boring very quickly. Syrus appears before the fleeing emperor, capturing his hair and baring his neck, the vampyr strikes like a viper. Draining every drop of blood within his body.

Syrus is sickened by the Emperor's actions. He is nothing more than a mere coward, seeking the easy way out, blaming others, bending over backwards to a deranged fool, but of course, for once, this fool is right. Syrus made it quick for him, as death is his greatest punishment. Dropping the body, another shadow appears near the corpse, bowing down to Syrus before disappearing into the darkness, waiting to be called.

The warlock only watches in horror, dread pooling to his stomach, his milky white eyes stare back at the vampyr and feeling warm tears streak down his wrinkled face.

"I – I knew it was you. You shouldn't have lived that day," he wheezes only to seal his fate. Syrus snarls, using his sheer strength. His clawed hands smacking the warlock's lower jaw, tearing the lower bone off its joints and flying halfway across the room, blood pools to onto the marble floors, only silent screams from the old man. A fitting way to start the slaughter. Syrus gently moves his hand over his chest, slowly stabbing his claws into the flesh and bone, grasping the vital organ within. Syrus gives a final smile and rips the fleshy organ out, blood pooling from the man's chest, the shadows drop the bleeding corpse. Crushing the organ within his hand, Syrus felt empty when committing the final act. He felt hollow. No longer did he feel satisfied with the kill. Nothing mattered to him anymore. Everything he cared about is gone.

***

The guards and people retaliated, and Syrus left the vampyrs to die, uncaring for their cries of help. He ignores the shadow's angry protest, cursing him, demanding to take his role as King, but he has no desire for it.

So here he is, sitting outside the city walls, in a small grass field, watching the sunset on a burning city. Syrus's hands returned to normal, no longer the terrifying claws he once had. They are still stained red from the blood of the people and his enemies.

Syrus gently rests his bloody hand on top of Annabeth's grave. "I'm sorry I turned out this way," He whispers. "I wonder what you would say if you saw me like this," he chuckles bitterly.

He hung his head to the ground, allowing the aching throb in his chest once more. "Would you be disgusted?

Would you run in terror, or would you forgive me?" Syrus asked the grave. Yearning to hear her reply, wishing he had some dark ability to speak with the dead, hoping he could see her one last time. Syrus weeps once more, curling into a ball, sobbing. "I'm sorry, I'm so sorry, Annabeth."

Syrus paid no attention to the footsteps behind him. No longer does he have the fight within him. He does not wish to remain in this world if his beloved is not in it. Syrus wants to die.

"I'm sorry, Syrus," Alexandros rasps, sitting next to the young man he raised.

"Please, Alexandros, end me," he cries, still hugging his legs and weeps. "I don't want to live in a world where she is not here. I don't to be a vampyr," Syrus sniffles. Hoping his words get through, but this time Alexandros lets his words fall on deaf ears.

"You made a choice, boy," he sighs, sitting himself up once more. "You had a chance to be better than them, a chance to walk away," he reiterates. "This is your punishment, Syrus. I won't kill you. Life will be your punishment." Syrus clenches his jaw, knowing this would happen. He chose revenge, and this will be his punishment. Life. "Enjoy your eternity of misery, Syrus."

Syrus no longer acknowledged the man who raised him. He just listens to the heavy steps disappear and lets the darkness shroud his huddled body, and the sun sinks into the horizon.

Frankish Empire, Cologne, 556 Common Era

It had been some time since Syrus had last visited Cologne. It has faired well since the collapse of the Roman empire. He found it amusing to watch his homeland fall upon itself. He even celebrated and treated himself to a meal. *When was the last I fed?* He thinks, ignoring the painful burn lingering in the back of this throat.

Syrus's grief has overwhelmed him for centuries since his awakening. It has destroyed his own will to live. He barely fed, ignoring the desperate need. It would become so unbearable, Syrus snaps and ravages towns, sating his extreme hunger.

But as time went on and his stubborn desire to die, Syrus has adapted to go longer and longer without feeding. There would be moments where he would sleep but only to be awakened by the shadows, forcing him to feed. This frustrated the vampyr, but he persisted.

Syrus no longer falls into a slumber. Instead, he is a walking starving corpse, able to control the ravaging hunger buried beneath his chest. No longer does he lose control of his desires.

Syrus walks through the quiet, dark streets, recognising the familiar scent of spilled blood in the air. Syrus acknowledges the blaze but bears no interest to feed.

The shadows are an odd anomaly, happy to do as they please and kill those who wish to endanger their master, regardless if he gave the order. They still listen to him, but there is the rare occasion when they ignore his protests in eating. He has learned to shut their relentless nattering amongst themselves. Only a few dare to speak to him directly when they wish to tell him things that might pique his interest.

Syrus hums to what one has to say as they whisper in his ear, interested in learning how this city controls its feral population. It makes sense why there is sweet blood spilled in this city tonight, only for it to turn horribly bitter and off.

Deciding to investigate, he follows the awful smell, mixed with the sweet scent. Syrus watches amongst the shadows, watching the hunters burn the feral corpses and cutting a human boy down from the wooden posts.

The boy collapses with a heavy thud, his heart barely beating at this point, his breathing shallows, movement is sluggish as he turns onto his back. Syrus watches in disbelief. Dread pools into the pit of his stomach, disgust filling his heart as he watches the hunters laugh at the child.

How dare they, he's just a boy! Anger flashed through him. A growl resonates beneath his chest, fangs digging into his lower lip. *Using a boy to lure monsters and abandoning him to die.*

The hunters leave him on the streets before Syrus could tear them apart. The anger only washes away, and he feels pity instead. The poor child was left alone to die.

Syrus doesn't think and moves closer to the dying boy, uncaring if hunters are still around.

A long incision is made along his gut. Blood pooling from the wound, not deep enough to kill him quickly but enough to gain ferals attention. His clothes are torn, dirty, and old. They barely fit him, his skin covered in grime, dirt, and now his own blood.

Concern only fills Syrus's mind and studies the boy more closely, but the boy frowns at Syrus, with his half-lidded eyes, struggling to keep himself awake. It was at this moment, without even thinking, Syrus opened his mouth and whispered these words.

"I can save you."

Social Media

Facebook: https://www.facebook.com/belindatopan
Twitter: https://twitter.com/BelindaTopan
Instagram: @belindatopan

Inkitt: www.inkitt.com/BelindaTopan
Wattpad: www.wattpad.com/user/BelindaTopan
Tapas: tapas.io/belindatopan

Books

Living With Vampires:
https://www.amazon.com.au/dp/B0842F1GK7

ILLUST BY PUPPYPAWW